Murderers' Row

The Second Sebastian McCabe — Jeff Cody Case Book

Dan Andriacco

Paperback ISBN 978-1-78705-606-0
ePub ISBN 978-1-78705-607-7
PDF ISBN 978-1-78705-608-4

Published in the UK by MX Publishing
335 Princess Park Manor, Royal Drive,
London, N11 3GX
www.mxpublishing.com
Cover design by Brian Belanger

I happily dedicate this book
(especially "Dead on the Fourth of July")
to my Sherlockian friends

Patty Bertsch
Ridgely Hunt
Marc Lehmann
S. Brent Morris
Bob Sharfman
Al Shaw
Daniel Stashower

and to the memory of

Professor Ben Sterling

—magicians all

CONTENTS

Before We Start

Dear Reader,

Welcome back! Or, if you are a newcomer to these precincts, welcome aboard!

Especially for the benefit of those making a return visit, Lynda, my better three-quarters, wanted me to clarify something upfront:

Up to now, I've been able to present these chronicles of Sebastian McCabe in the order in which they happened. The current volume, however, includes what I think of as "in-fill." The cases here recorded as "A Destination Murder" and "Dead on the Fourth of July" both happened before the events of the most recent book, *Too Many Clues*. To see when the primary action of each installment of the series takes place, please consult the chronology at the back of this book. I may need to consult it myself as memory fades.

By the way, all the Barbados locations mentioned in "A Destination Murder" are real, although in some cases the names are not.

Why the delay in publishing the following cases? They were less complicated than most of Mac's exploits, and therefore shorter to tell. So, as with the first Sebastian McCabe-Jeff Cody case book, *Rogues Gallery*, I waited until I had several such shorter accounts to put them together between the covers of a book. I hope you'll agree they were worth the wait.

—*Jeff Cody*

A Destination Murder

I

Murder and matrimony shouldn't mix, but nobody planned it that way—not even the murderer.

The news that our friends Maureen "Mo" Russert and Jonathan Hawes planned to end their long engagement by tying the proverbial knot in Barbados—and on St. Valentine's Day, no less—elicited only mild interest on my part when Lynda broke the news over breakfast one morning. At first, I didn't even look up from the Saturday *Wall Street Journal*.

The S&P 500 Index had gone crazy that fall in the aftermath of the just-concluded 2016 election. Even for a long-term investor like me, that caused a few stomach-flutters. But by the beginning of December, when this conversation took place, the S&P stood at two-and-a-half times where it was at the Great Recession low point in 2008. The only people losing money in the market were the short sellers, speculators who bet on stocks to go down. All this was going through my head when Lynda followed her initial announcement about the nuptials with:

"A destination wedding on a Caribbean island paradise. Don't you think that's just so romantic?"

Assuming she was talking to me, not our infant daughter in the high-chair, I responded.

"Uh-huh." *Maybe I should rebalance our asset allocation now instead of waiting until the end of the quarter.*

"I'll need to buy a new outfit, of course, something bright and island-y."

"Uh-huh." *But the end of the quarter is only—wait a minute!* I put down the *WSJ*. "What are you talking about, Lyn?"

"The wedding. Barbados. St. Valentine's Day. Pay attention, darling." Lynda Teal Cody, my wife and the love of my life, pouted prettily. So, I paid attention. Oval face, olive skin, gold-flecked brown eyes, cutely crooked nose, a head of honey blond curls—suddenly I was having romantic thoughts that had nothing to do with somebody else's wedding. With some effort, I dragged the Cody concentration back to the subject at hand.

"I was listening." *You had me at "buy."* "But I think you skipped a few of the dots. What does the Russert-Hawes wedding have to do with you?"

"I'm Mo's matron of honor. Didn't I tell you that?"

"No!"

"Really? I thought sure I did. Well, I am. I was honored to be asked. And Mac's the best man."

"What? Why him?"

"Well, he does have experience at that particular gig. Remember our wedding?"

"Vividly." Meaning I recalled Lynda's mother, and the horrors of her pre-wedding antics[1] as well as the fun parts, like seeing Mac in a tux and dancing with Lynda to the songs of Sinatra.

"Besides, he's Mo's business partner," Lynda added. My brother-in-law and Mo own Mo's Mysteries & Marvels bookstore together, with Mac as the supposedly silent partner. Jonathan, for his part, owns Hawes & Holder, Erin, Ohio's premier funeral home. "And it all works out perfectly because Mac has a good friend in Barbados. Some Sherlockian muckety muck." No surprise there; Sebastian

---

[1] See *The 1895 Murder* (MX Publishing, 2012).

McCabe has friends everywhere, many of them sharing his childish passion for the character they often call the Great Detective or simply the Master.

A suspicion dawned on me. "Was Barbados your idea?" I asked.

What I knew about the island was restricted to a few beautiful images from the James Bond movie *Dragonfly*, which the movie star Heather O'Toole was filming during the murder of her super-rich husband.[2] And HO'T, as the tabloids invariably called her, and my beloved spouse had become friends of sorts during our time in London.

"Don't be silly. That was Mo's brainstorm."

"But February's just around the corner. Weddings are usually planned months in advance. Why the rush? She isn't—"

"No, she isn't. I don't think. She just decided it's time. And it's going to be a very small wedding, just us chickens, so the planning is no big deal."

Mo is a good egg, a real sweetheart who got a raw deal when her stuffy first husband, one Arthur Bancroft Russert, left her and their two daughters for another woman. He paid his alimony and child support on time and was dutiful to the girls, though, according to Mo. That made the break-up relatively easy—except for a hole it left in Mo's heart. The couple of times I took her out in my bachelor days, during a four-week period in which Lynda and I were on pause in our relationship, made it clear I wasn't the man to fill that hole. That turned out to be Jonathan's role.

"This destination wedding thing is all very well for the bride and groom, but it sounds expensive," I objected. "That will still be the high season in the Caribbean. And what do we do with Donata?" I wasn't worried about my two McCabe nieces and their brother. Being in their teens and extraordinarily responsible, they could fend for themselves

---

[2] See *The Disappearance of Mr. James Phillimore* (MX Publishing, 2013).

for a few days, with occasional help. But our daughter wasn't quite fourteen months old. She looked up from her Cheerios at the mention of her name, seemingly puzzled, but no more so than me. The day had just begun, and I was already losing control. As usual.

Lynda left Donata's side, came up behind me, and put her arms around me. The scent of Cleopatra VII perfume lingered on her from the night before.

"Mac's mom said she'd be happy to move in for a few days. Let's take advantage of that while we can. She may not be so eager when we have more kiddos." We would, in fact, have two more less than a year later, but we didn't know it at the time. "Think of this as a second honeymoon, *tesoro mio*." The suggestion was whispered in my ear in a way that gave me goose bumps. Lynda's throaty voice was at its throaty-est. But Jeff Cody is not that easily distracted in mid-grump.

"Second honeymoon, eh?" I said. "You do remember that there was a murder during our first honeymoon, don't you?"

"And that's a great reason for a do-over! I mean, nothing like that's going to happen this time, right?"

II

A couple of months later, on Friday, February 10, we stepped off a Jet Blue plane at Grantley Adams International Airport in Bridgetown, the capital of Barbados. The temperature was in the mid-eighties, more than thirty degrees higher than what we left behind in Ohio.

"Who turned on the heat in this country?" my sister Kate asked. A week earlier, she'd been griping about the cold and asking if winter would never end.

Fortunately, we were all dressed for the islands. Even Mac had clothed his immense girth in a short-sleeved shirt with a palm tree design, worn with the shirt tail out. It wasn't a pretty sight.

Barbadians, I learned from *Frommer's*, are commonly called Bajans. Mac's Bajan friend, who met us at the gate, was a tall, distinguished-looking black gent with white hair. I found out later he was eighty-one, but with baby-smooth skin he looked more than a decade younger.

"Mac, old friend!" he exclaimed, making a futile attempt to put his arms around the big guy. He spoke with an accent that sounded to me more Scottish than the English variety you hear in Jamaica. I won't attempt to convey it phonetically here.

"Sir Owen, it has been far too long," Mac said.

The Bajan hastily introduced himself to the rest of us: "Owen Cumberbatch, at your service."

"Cumberbatch?" Lynda blurted.

Sir Owen smiled broadly. "It's the most common surname on the island. There are even some whites named Cumberbatch up north. Forgive my lack of originality."

"Lynda is quite the fan of a certain Sherlockian actor of that name," Mac informed him. I was staying out of it.

"Many young women are, I understand. Benedict Cumberbatch is that gentleman's real name from birth. His ancestors were pioneering plantation owners here going back to the seventeenth century. They had many slaves, which is why the name is so widespread."

The four of us—Mo and Jonathan had arrived the day before but didn't come to the airport to greet us—piled into Sir Owen's red Honda CRV.

"They call us Little England, you know," he said as we tooled through the capital city.

"Is that why you have that statue of Lord Nelson, like the one in Trafalgar Square?" I pointed.

"Actually, ours came first—by almost thirty years."

Oh.

"And the square it dominates here was also called Trafalgar, but the name was changed almost twenty years ago to National Heroes Square."

Sir Owen drove fast through the narrow streets (and on the wrong side), but so did everybody else. I was all eyes as he sped us to our hotel on the Atlantic Ocean side of the 166-square-mile island. The flowers were so full and waxy they looked artificial. Women dressed to the nines in colorful dresses walked along the side of the road—there were no sidewalks—carrying umbrellas against the heat of the sun. Men played dominos, sitting at little tables outside of shack-like buildings decorated with signs for Banks beer, Mount Gay Rum, or even Guinness.

"The fabled rum shops, are they not?" Mac rumbled.

"Oh, yes," Sir Owen confirmed. "And when the patrons get drunk, they sing Anglican hymns. I hope you don't mind that I took the liberty of buying you tickets to the Hazel Carter concert tomorrow night."

"Here?" I won't say that Lynda shrieked like a teenager. But she did. Hazel Carter had just exploded onto the pop music scene the year before, quickly attracting an international fandom known as Hazelnuts. She was the most famous Bajan entertainer since Rihanna.

Sir Owen nodded. "It's a big charity event for babies born addicted to drugs. Half the residents of the island will be there, and just about all the tourists. Hazelnuts are coming from all over the map. I jumped on the tickets as soon as they became available."

"I suspect that Sir Owen pulled some strings," Mac, riding shotgun, told Kate with a knowing wink.

"Thank you, Sir Owen," she said. "How incredibly thoughtful."

Lynda leaned forward from the back seat. "So, what line of work are you in, Sir Owen?"

"Oh, I'm a retired dabbler. I was an economics professor at the University of the West Indies, and a business consultant, which got me on the boards of a few companies. And then I did a bit of writing for the *Nation*, our biggest newspaper. Then, finally, I reached my level of incompetency by falling into a government job."

"To be specific," Mac said, "Sir Owen was until recently the Governor-General of Barbados, meaning he was the official representative of Her Majesty the Queen. The position comes with a title and a residence called Government House." *Not too shabby.* "However, that pales next to Sir Owen's accomplishments as a scholar of detective fiction, particularly that of the Golden Age and all things Sherlock Holmes."

I filed that assessment of relative importance under *Mac's Peculiar Perspectives.*

"Wow. Is there anything you haven't done?" Lynda exclaimed.

Sir Owen thought a moment. "Omelets. I tried once, but my breakfast cooking skills are sadly deficient. Also, I am sad to say I have never solved a murder, unlike our distinguished friend here." Mac preened, although he probably thought he was looking modest. "I must admit that's a secret ambition of mine, solving a murder—although I doubt that will ever happen."

Also, it's no longer a secret.

I went back to looking at the scenery.

"What's with all those small wooden houses?" I asked. There were a lot of them dotting the landscape when we got out of Bridgetown, many in bad shape.

"They're called chattel houses, and they date back to plantation days in Barbados. What makes them distinctive is that they are made of wood, not concrete block, and they have no nails so that they can be easily disassembled and moved to another property. Working-class people owned them, but they didn't own the land. So, if they had a dispute with the landlord, usually the owner of the plantation where they worked, they could pick up the house and move it. Even though many have fallen apart, the island still has thousands. Some have been added to over the years to be much bigger than they began."

Housing always interests me, so I asked why so many of the newer concrete block houses were unpainted or only partially painted.

Sir Owen smiled. "If they aren't painted, they aren't finished. And if they aren't finished, the property taxes on them are lower."

Clever, these Bajans!

"I noticed a lot of men in dreadlocks," Kate said. "Are they all Rastafarians?"

The old man sobered up. "Not necessarily. That hairstyle is now generally popular. But we do still have our share of Rastas. You may associate them with smoking cannabis, and rightly so, but they are not entirely responsible for the regrettable amount of drug smuggling on the island—especially weed, but also cocaine."

In far less time than it took us to drive from Erin to the airport in Cleveland for our Jet Blue flight, we were on the other side of the island—the east coast. Sir Owen dropped us off at our destination of Naniki in the parish of St. Joseph. (The island is divided into eleven parishes, or counties, each of which has an Anglican church of that name.) Naniki is a complex that includes a wellness center (with ozone therapy!) and a restaurant as well as our cottages. The happy couple were also staying at Naniki, and already in residence a few cottages away from the adjoining Cody and McCabe abodes.

Not wanting to crash in on the lovebirds, and in need of a nap herself after a long day of travel, Lynda called Mo's cell from Sir Owen's car. She arranged for us to meet up with the bride-to-be and Jonathan for dinner. Sir Owen recommended the fish fry at Oistins Bay Gardens, well-known to both visitors and locals.

We arrived at Oistins, a fishing town on the south coast, at about 5:45 that evening. The four of us strolled along the pier, two couples holding hands, and watched a spectacular sunset. Lynda put her head on my shoulder.

"Worth it?" she asked me.

"Absolutely." *You can't buy a sunset.*

Oistins Bay Gardens is a bit on the rustic side, with open-air dining at long tables and old-timers playing dominos. All manner of fish, grilled or fried depending on the vendor you chose, was cooked on the spot.

"Utterly charming," Mac proclaimed it.

I choked back a knee-jerk dissenting view because, in truth, he was right. Not only that, the place was real, not just a tourist production, although there were plenty of tourists among the natives. As we walked around, I caught snippets of the locals speaking Bajan creole, sounding not at all like Sir Owen:

"Wuna eat de fish?"
"Dat no hobby class!"
"De higher de monkey climb, de more he show he tail."

It took us awhile to spot Mo and Jonathan amongst the revelers.

Maureen Russert is a couple of years older than me, in her mid-forties at the time of the wedding, but she didn't look it that night. Her freckled face glowed and her dark bangs glistened. Jonathan Hawes, whose height and facial architecture made him a perfect Sherlock Holmes in Mac's *1895* play a few years earlier, looked at her—well, the way I look at Lynda.

Lynda grabbed Mo. "This is so exciting!" Hugs ensued, although I only shook Jonathan's hand.

"Thank you for doing this," Mo said to Lynda and Mac. "Thanks to all of you."

"I couldn't miss it," I said. *I wasn't allowed to.*

The live calypso band made conversation a bit of a challenge. But we managed to catch up while we downed among us swordfish, marlin, mahi-mahi, and the Bajan signature treat of flying fish (grilled for me). Not to mention the multiple bottles of Banks beer consumed by Mac.

"The trip was fine," Kate reported, "and Sir Owen gave us a little tour on our way to Naniki."

"Jonathan and I haven't seen much of the island," Mo said. *I bet!* "We were waiting for you guys."

"How are your girls?" Lynda asked.

"Still a little peeved that I'm doing this without them." Her frown passed like a shadow over the moon. "All this came up rather quickly. We just couldn't work it around their school and work schedules. We'll make it up to them somehow."

Jonathan took her hand. "I'm sure we will. But I'm not sorry to be honeymooning alone."

I guess he forgot we were there.

"I'm so happy," Mo said. "Nothing could spoil this."

III

"Perhaps I should set a mystery novel in Barbados," Mac mused the next morning over a hearty breakfast of coconut bakes, scrambled eggs, sautéed green bananas, and fresh fruit. If we kept eating like this, the women would have to let out their dresses for the wedding.

"Great idea," I told Mac. "Then you can write off the cost of this trip as a business expense."

"You won't lack for material," Lynda said, looking up from *The Saturday Sun*. As a journalist by blood, she shares my habit of reading the local newspaper wherever we are. "I see what Sir Owen meant about the marijuana trade. There's a big story in here about a Jamaican lawyer in Barbados who makes a living representing her countrymen charged with smuggling. And then there's story about police corruption."

I was more taken by the British slang in the startling headline: **ACCUSED: IT'S A LIE, I DID NOT BUGGER HIM.**

"That is not my sort of crime, as I am sure you realize," Mac said, referring to the smuggling, not the buggering. "The murders in my novels are all the work of amateurs, as is the sleuthing." He stroked his graying beard thoughtfully. "Of course, a novel also needs subplots and red herrings."

"Don't you ever stop working?" Kate grumbled.

"I presume that is a rhetorical question, my dear."

"I'm glad Jonathan doesn't work all the time," Mo said.

Her fiancé put a theatrical glower on his lean face. "Is that an undertaker joke? You know how I hate undertaker jokes."

"Oh, look at this cute video of Donata that Mac's mom sent!" Lynda held out her phone.

After breakfast, at Sir Owen's suggestion, we drove up the east coast just a bit and spent a few hours overdosing on the floral beauty of the Andromeda Botanical Gardens in the village of Bathsheba. Another kind of beauty was on display when we donned swimsuits and sunscreen to walk along the beach for a while. (Heavy on the sun blockers for my blond wife and for Kate and me, both red-headed.) The waves were too strong for swimming along the rugged coastline, but I loved the roar of the Atlantic. I also loved the one-piece aquamarine suit that hugged Lynda's exquisite figure. Mercifully, Mac eschewed swimming trunks and stuck with his shorts and short-sleeved shirt.

"The ocean air certainly enhances one's appetite," he commented.

Before I could point out that in my experience a flagging appetite had never been one of his problems, Jonathan said, "What was the name of the place you wanted to go for lunch, honey?"

"The Historic Aquarius Inn," Mo said. "It's famous."

Better yet, it was nearby in Bathsheba. Lunching on the outside deck, the six of us shared an appetizer tray of fish cakes. I followed up with a swordfish sandwich. I don't eat a lot of red meat, and even less in sight of an ocean, but my luncheon mates stood in the gap on that.

"I could use a nap," Lynda said as we polished off the last of it.

Well, all right! Naps in the Cody household usually don't involve only sleeping. But before I could pick up on Lynda's comment by suggesting that we go back to our cottage, Mo said, "Well, look who the cat dragged in!" She spoke rather loudly in a tone I interpreted as surprise. I later

learned that it wasn't, not by a long shot. I followed her
eyes—or rather, her sunglasses. She was looking at two men
and two women approaching an empty table with the clear
intention of occupying it for lunch.

"That is your former husband, is it not?" Mac asked.

"Oh, yes." She smiled.

Well, this is a bit awkward.

I couldn't have picked Arthur Bancroft Russert out
of a lineup. After he dumped Mo, he moved to Cincinnati
and I never had the questionable pleasure of meeting him.
Therefore, I didn't know whether he was the powerfully built
guy with the broad face and high forehead or the more
handsome article with a head of thick brown hair, carefully
parted on the left, and a square jaw. But the latter didn't leave
me in the dark long. His eyebrows shot up and the blue eyes
below them widened.

"Mo!"

"Hello, Arthur dear." The tone of her voice was
somewhat colder than the ice in my glass of Caffeine-Free
Diet Coke.

The woman standing closest to Russert was a petite
blonde, with her hair brushing the tops of her shoulders.
From what I could see of her face through a pair of roundish,
pink glasses, she wasn't somebody you'd notice in a crowd.
Around her neck hung a Canon digital camera with a
telephoto lens, something you don't see so often now that
phones are smart enough to take pictures with. Her brightly
colored dress, short with a low back, looked like something
bought on the island.

"What are you doing here?" Russert asked the ex-
Mrs. Russert.

Mo smiled like a cartoon cat with canary feet sticking
out of his mouth. "We're staying at Naniki. And on
Valentine's Day I'm getting married to someone I love." She
grabbed Jonathan's nearby arm. "You should try it
sometime."

"I knew you were getting remarried, of course, but I never—Well, anyway," he stammered, "you look great. I hope everything works out well for you."

"I'm sure it will for *you*, Art—no more alimony."

I so want to not be here.

The blonde stepped forward and put out her hand. "Mrs. Russert? I'm Sabrina Coe. We've never actually met."

"No, Arthur managed to keep us apart while he was married to me and seeing you." (I cleaned that up a little.) "That was the one thing he was good at. I thought you'd have bigger boobs. Please call me Mo. I'm dropping the Russert in three days.[3] Better late than never."

This is going well.

"I'm very happy for you," Sabrina Coe said. She didn't look all that flat-chested to me. "Really, I am, Mo."

The look on Mo's face was hard to read—at least by me—but she didn't make another snappy retort.

"Oh, look at the time," Kate said, not looking at her watch or phone. "We'd better be going."

"Indeed," Mac thundered.

Sounded good to me, even though we had no place to be for hours.

"It was so nice to meet you," said the other woman in the Russert party. Her smile, the product of a generous mouth, took the edge off what had to be sarcasm, considering that we hadn't been introduced. She was short and so was her hair, a stunning shade of grey-white even though she couldn't have been older than the low-forties. That hair nagged at my memory. Where had I seen her before? If she were thirty pounds or so overweight, that didn't stop her from wearing cut-off jeans and a lacy white top. She looked like a bundle of energy just standing there.

---

[3] She didn't, though. For professional reasons, she is still Mo Russert today.

"Sorry," Russert mumbled, clearly getting the point of the dig. He presented his friends, Marcus and Cricket Wagner.

"*Shark Tank*!" I said, without waiting for Mo to dole out our names in return.

Lynda had that "can't take you anywhere" look on her face, but Cricket Wagner said, "That's right."

I'd seen her on the show a year or so earlier with a portable diaper-changing apparatus that she'd invented for use with her own three children.

"Great invention you had there!" I told her. "I'm sorry none of the sharks invested in your business."

"Oh, don't be! Business is booming from the publicity, and I didn't have to take in a partner."

Mo cut short this fascinating (to me, anyway) discussion by introducing the rest of us to Russert and his traveling companions. Jonathan tried to be cordial, and why not? Russert's loss was his gain.

"How long are you going to be in Barbados?" Lynda asked.

"Not too much longer," Russert said.

The Hazel Carter concert was "awesome!" So said Lynda as we ate world-class ice cream afterwards (rum raisin for me) at a fast food restaurant called Chefette. Somehow, my wife had turned from a mere fan into a certified Hazelnut since landing on the island. She bought a concert T-shirt to prove it. My sister didn't yell and gyrate insanely during the event like Lynda did, but she used the word "fabulous" in describing it later. Mac, who in his spare time runs St. Benignus University's small popular culture program, pontificated on the "popular" and "cultural" aspects of the concert experience, laced with observations about Ms. Carter's appeal to women of a certain age range. That was brave, given the presence of Kate and Lynda.

As for my own reaction to the concert, I couldn't understand the words of songs I'd never heard before, and that always makes me suspicious. Also, my mind was somewhat occupied during the performance by mixed thoughts of the day's events. Mo had been clever, witty—and nasty. Not like her usual pleasant self at all. But maybe that's normal for a woman who encounters her ex-husband and the woman who replaced her in his life.

Anyway, I was somewhat quiet during the concert post-mortem at Chefette, even when not eating. Then Lynda and I parted from Mac and Kate to walk on the beach by ourselves. The waves roiled in the moonlight and Lynda put her head on my shoulder.

"Isn't this romantic, *tesoro mio?*"

"Romantic" was the word she'd used months before to describe this destination wedding, whereas I would have chosen "expensive." But at that moment—

"I couldn't agree more," I whispered.

After a few minutes of exploring that topic, we strolled back to our cottage. Not fast enough for me!

Some minutes after getting in, we heard a knock on the door. We were in the shower.

"No, no, no!" I snarled. "Who would be knocking on our door at this time of night?"

"A friend in need," said Lynda, always compassionate as well as comely.

"Oh."

We grabbed bathrobes, put them on, and opened the cottage door. It was Mo, looking like a politician the day after an election defeat. Even her cute bangs seemed to droop.

"Sorry to bother you," she said. "In fact, maybe I'd better—"

"Come on in," Lynda said. "We weren't going to bed any time soon." *I thought we were.* "We're still winding down from the concert. It was incredible. Here, have some rum."

When in Barbados . . .

"Thanks."

While Lynda poured, I ducked back into the bathroom with my clothes and got a little more dressed. I came back into the room to find Mo in mid-explanation.

". . . but I didn't hate her at all! How could I? She seemed genuinely nice to me. I thought she would be a rich bitch. She inherited a pile from her parents, who were liquor distributors. That's how Art met her—he manages her money. But I just Googled her name for the first time. It turns out she runs a non-profit making micro-loans for poor people to start businesses here in the Caribbean! She's not the sort of person I thought at all. I feel so ashamed."

"Having unkind thoughts about people isn't a crime, thank heavens," Lynda. "We all do that, from time to time."

"And you didn't exactly unsheathe your talons on *her*," I added with a chuckle. *Except for that crack about her body shape.* "You saved that for your ex. So, don't be so upset with yourself. You have no reason to be."

"Yes, I do."

She closed her eyes and took a healthy slug of Old Brigand Barbados Rum neat. I prefer mine mixed with Caffeine-Free Diet Coke, and not too much of it. I don't expect to live forever, but I would like to outlive my liver.

"I could never tell Jonathan this," Mo said, "and you can't tell him either."

"Tell him what?" Lynda asked.

"I picked this island at this time because I knew Art and Sabrina were going to be here. Jonathan has no idea that's why we rushed the wedding."

"How in the world did you know—"

"You'd be surprised how many 'friends' are eager to tell you about your ex's wonderful life. One of them even told me that Art and Sabrina were staying at the Aquarius. That's why I picked it for lunch. But now I see how stupid it was to come all this way just to try to ruin Art's vacation by rubbing it in his face that I'm marrying a better man than him."

"Your feelings toward a despicable man who ran out on you four years ago are entirely understandable," Lynda said.

Should I get my testosterone-infested body out of here?

"I don't really hate him, you know, any more than I hate Sabrina," Mo clarified. "There was something real between us once. At least, I thought it was real. Maybe it was just those eyes, those beautiful blue eyes and his charm. He did have charm. I guess he still does. Apparently, he's charmed Sabrina for years." She sighed and worked on the rum for a bit. "He gave me two wonderful daughters. I'll always be grateful for that. And when you share children, you stay in each other's lives.

"I'm not proud that I watched with secret satisfaction when that trendy Cincinnati restaurant that Art invested in went bankrupt last year. But that wasn't enough for me. Oh, no, I had to drag Jonathan here for our wedding just because I thought it would upset Art. And I'm not even sure it did. I was such a fool!" Tears threatened.

"No, you're being a fool now, Mo." The motherly way Lynda spoke, one would have thought she was the older woman instead of the reverse. "It doesn't matter how you got here. You're going to have a wonderful wedding on Tuesday and a great marriage."

Mo sat back, a hint of a smile on her face. "You seem pretty sure about my life."

"I am."

"Everything will look better in the morning," I assured Mo. "You'll see."

IV

In the morning, Sunday, Sir Owen took us into Bridgetown—"us" being a party of five.

"Mo doesn't feel well," Jonathan said, "but she told me to come with you guys."

Our first stop was the early Mass at St. Patrick's Cathedral. The church is appropriately big, with a high vaulted ceiling, arched windows, and stained glass. The windows were open, and birds flew freely throughout. It was hard for me to keep in mind that it was Abraham Lincoln's birthday, with the temperature about 40 degrees back home.

Spirituality taken care of, we went on to spirits at Mount Gay distillery. It's the world's oldest distiller of rum, "Est. 1703," as the sign says. We toured the facility and tasted the product, though not to excess. Then Kate dragged us to Pelican Village, a collection of small wood-frame shops on the outskirts of the city selling local handicrafts. Every time I heard Lynda exclaim, "Oh, how cute!" I knew the Cody credit card was in for a workout. "Christmas gifts," she explained. But we kept for ourselves a nice black-and-white block print of Bajan fishermen casting their nets. It hangs above my desk as I write this.

Rain paid a visit just as we came out of the last colorfully painted shop, Lynda and Kate each clutching several bulging bags. But the sun didn't go away.

"Barbados has only two seasons—sunny and rainy," Sir Owen informed us. "It is not unusual to have both at the same time. We like to say the sun and the rain are getting married."

Passing the bronze statue of Admiral Lord Nelson in National Heroes Square, we went to lunch at the nearby Nelson's Arms Pub. I felt like I was back in jolly old England, what with the standard-issue British pub interior. But Jonathan didn't look so jolly.

"You seem distracted," Mac observed between quaffs of Banks beer.

"Is that what you call it! Wouldn't you be a little off your feed if you were in my shoes? A guy about to get married in a tropical paradise doesn't expect to run into a snake in the garden."

"Well, there is a precedent for that. You refer, of course, to Mo's former husband and the father of her children."

He winced. "Some father. He spends time with them, but everything else I know about him says he's a selfish schmuck. What kind of example is that for the girls?"

"Forget about him," Lynda said. "I'm sure Mo has."

"I wonder about that," Jonathan said, in no way cheered by this unburdening of soul.

Just then his phone pinged. He looked down and smiled. "It's a text from Mo. She wants us to circle back and pick her up."

We did so.

At Harrison's Caves, we and a bunch of British tourists took a tram ride through a limestone cavern. After a little beach time followed by a snooze, we dined at the Sandpiper Hotel, where the cocktails are expensive, but everybody gets a free coconut and the bartender opens it for you. Mac called that "novel."

"This trip is going too fast, just like every vacation," Lynda told me the next morning. "I can't believe the wedding is tomorrow already."

"That's no sweat for you," I reminded her. "All you have to do is relax and look beautiful. It's in the bag!"

She kissed me, not making a rush job of it.

Sir Owen stopped by right after breakfast to take us to the Barbados Wildlife Reserve in the northern parish of St. Peter. It was a delightful way to spend a workless Monday morning, even though I did get shoved by a small green monkey. The wild hares there have long legs that make them look like tiny deer.

We went back to grab our bathing suits for some quality time with the white sand and turquoise water of Paynes Bay on the west coast, but that never happened. Standing in front of Mo and Jonathan's cottage, strongly resembling a refrigerator in size and build, stood a Bajan man with close-cropped hair. And I thought: *Even in short sleeves all cops look alike.* What I said to my companions was:

"This can't be good."

"All my parking fines are paid," Sir Owen muttered, as if to himself.

Our visitor didn't have parking infractions on his mind.

"Is one of you the former Mrs. Maureen Russert?" he asked.

She admitted it.

"I am Inspector Mervin Brathwaite of the Royal Barbados Police Force. I would like to ask you a few questions, informally at this point."

Sir Owen stepped forward. "May I ask why, Inspector?"

"Sir Owen!" I can't say that he turned pale, but he was startled to realize that the former Governor-General of Barbados was among our company. ("I don't know everyone in the country," Sir Owen later told me, "but everyone seems to know me. That's not always a good thing.")

"Why?" the venerable statesman repeated.

Brathwaite pulled himself together. "Another American, a woman named Sabrina Coe, was strangled to death yesterday afternoon in the room she shared with Mrs.

Russert's former husband. He and another couple with whom they were traveling found the body upon returning to the hotel from sightseeing."

Nobody said anything. Not even "What!" I think we were all struggling to process it. Mo gripped Jonathan's hand and squeezed it until her own hand turned white. Her mouth hung open. Finally, Mac said, "That is very disturbing news indeed. How may we be of assistance to the police?"

Not the way you hope, I bet.

"My questions are for Mrs. Russert," Brathwaite said. *Translation: "Butt out."* He turned slightly more Mo's way to emphasize the point. "Did Ms. Coe break up your marriage to Mr. Russert?"

"She—" Mo paused, then shook her head. "No, no she didn't, not really. It was already broken before Art met that poor woman. I only recently realized that. I'm sorry it took me so long. But I've been divorced almost four years now and I came to Barbados to get married." She looked up at Jonathan. He extracted his hand and put his arm around her as she continued: "I didn't really know Sabrina Coe, Inspector. I only met her for the first time the other day, Saturday. But I'm sorry that she's dead. That's awful."

I was afraid that Brathwaite would question the convenience of Mo's appearance on a small Caribbean island at the same time her ex-husband and his girlfriend vacationed here, but he had other flying fish to fry:

"Mr. Russert tells me that you visited Ms. Coe yesterday at their hotel."

"That's not true!" Jonathan said.

"I'm so sorry," Mo told him.

"About what?"

But Mo answered Brathwaite, not her fiancé. "It's true. I did meet Sabrina for coffee at the Aquarius's restaurant in mid-morning, while Jonathan and our friends were out at church and seeing various sights. I suppose I should explain that our encounter on Saturday left me more than a little unsettled in retrospect—I'd behaved quite rudely, while she was more than civil in return. I wanted to apologize, so I went to see her."

If it's possible to stagger without moving, Jonathan did that. The expression on his face while Mo spoke was hard to read. Shock? Disbelief? Hurt? Maybe all of the above.

"Mr. Russert said you talked with Ms. Cole for some time, perhaps half an hour."

"That's about right, I guess. I didn't time it."

"What did you talk about?"

"I told you, I wanted to tell her I was sorry."

Brathwaite's wide face registered skepticism. "And that took so long?"

Mo almost smiled. "I also suggested during our conversation that Art Russert was not a man to be trusted, based on my long experience. I reminded her that he'd been unfaithful to me. It's only common sense that a man who cheats on one partner is quite capable of doing it to another."

"And she reacted negatively?"

"No! Not at all. I was so surprised! She expressed regret for being 'the other woman' in my breakup with Art, and she told me my warning was appreciated but unnecessary." Mo paused. "The funny thing is, though, she said she knew for a fact that he was 'faithful as a dog, but still a dog.' Her exact words. I gathered that their relationship was on the rocks and he was trying to salvage it with this trip, but no luck."

"Are you trying to cast suspicion on Mr. Russert?" Brathwaite asked.

"What? Oh, hell no. I don't think Art would hurt anybody—not physically."

Sebastian McCabe broke his unaccustomed silence with a theatrical throat-clearing aimed Brathwaite's way. "Surely a simple burglary gone horribly wrong is the most obvious explanation for this sad situation," he said.

Brathwaite regarded him, not kindly. "And you are?"

Mac looked in silent appeal at Sir Owen, who didn't need a brick to fall on his head to get the message.

"This is my friend Sebastian McCabe," the great man informed Brathwaite. "He is quite familiar with police investigations, being something of an amateur Nero Wolfe." *At least the size is right.* "He has been of great help to his local constabulary, and even Scotland Yard, in solving several murders."

The Bajan gendarme turned falsely jovial. "Oh, I am sure we won't need any outside help solving a simple matter of burglary."

Touché! Suddenly, I'm liking this guy.

Sir Owen ignored the policeman's sarcasm—or was it irony? Hard to tell, but there was an attitude there, for sure.

"Nevertheless, Inspector, I would appreciate it if you would extend Professor McCabe every courtesy. And I'm sure my friend Commissioner Small would be grateful as well."

But no pressure.

"Of course, Sir Owen. You had a comment, Mr. McCabe?"

This was like dangling raw meat over the head of a lion.

"I did," Mac said. "Now I have a question: Do any facts of the case argue against the theory that the victim discovered a burglary in process and was killed as a result?" *Other than the fact that murder by local talent would be bad for the tourist trade, as opposed to tourist-on-tourist violence.*

"I should like to know the answer to that myself," Sir Owen offered.

"There was no forced entry," the inspector said. "That is somewhat unusual in a burglary, but not unknown. There were signs of a struggle in the room and several of Ms. Cole's personal items were taken, according to Mr. Russert. Of course, an intelligent killer with a personal motive might have staged a robbery as what they call in mystery novels a red herring."

Jonathan glowered.

"What sort of personal items were taken?" Mac wanted to know.

"Laptop, camera, jewelry—Mr. Russert supplied a list."

"Those are all items that a thief can fence without too much trouble. What about her cell phone?"

"We have that."

"That could be helpful."

"We expect so, Mr. McCabe. Speaking of cell phones, may I have your number, Mrs. Russert?"

"Of course." She supplied it.

"Thank you. What are your plans for the next few days?"

"I'm supposed to be getting married tomorrow."

"And after that?"

"We planned to honeymoon here in Barbados for another week and a half."

"Good. Please don't leave the country without letting me know." He gave her his card.

"I'll be responsible for making sure that she doesn't," Sir Owen said. "Staying close to this charming couple will be a pleasant duty. In fact, I was already planning on it. I am officiating at the wedding ceremony."

"Very well, then. Thank you, Sir Owen."

Believe it or not, he left without asking whether Mac had any further questions.

"What do you mean *supposed* to get married, Mo?" Jonathan asked his bride-to-be. "Are you in any doubt?"

"No, of course not. That was just a figure of speech."

"Is that what it was when you told us you didn't feel well yesterday?"

"I didn't feel well! I felt awful about the way I acted to Sabrina at the Aquarius. That's not who I am."

The cliché grated on my ear, but that didn't mean it was untrue.

"We'll leave you two love birds to work this out," Lynda said. "I'm sure you will."

Jonathan Hawes's bachelor party that evening consisted of meeting Mac and me at a rum shop sponsored by Banks, "the beer of Barbados."

Mac pulled out one of his enormous (not to mention ruinously expensive) Antonio de la Cova cigars and ordered a pitcher of the local brew. And that was just for him.

"Wedding still on?" I asked Jonathan, in what I hope was a joking tone.

"As long as Mo can stay out of jail," he replied gloomily.

"Everything will look better in the morning," I assured him. "You'll see."

V

In the morning, Jonathan and Mo's wedding day, *The Daily Nation* splashed **HEIRESS KILLED** across the top of the paper, with the four-deck subhead *Tourist Strangled in Aquarius Inn Hotel Room*.

"I guess 'heiress' is technically true, but she wasn't exactly Gloria Vanderbilt," Lynda kibitzed. "And what a long lead sentence!" She can't just read a newspaper; she has to edit it.

A two-column-wide glamour shot of Sabrina Coe, looking much more striking than the woman we had met, accompanied the story by reporter Jaydene Robinson. It made for awful breakfast-table reading, never mind the delightful island breeze and the soundtrack provided by the waves of the Atlantic in the distance beyond the trees:

> Sabrina Coe, 37, an American tourist who inherited a multi-million-dollar fortune and established a non-profit organization making micro-loans to female entrepreneurs in the Caribbean and Latin America, was found dead Sunday at her room in the Historic Aquarius Inn in Bathsheba. She had been strangled.
>
> "This is just devastating," said her romantic partner, Arthur Russert, who found the body. "I really can't talk about it. I have no words."
>
> Ms. Coe, Russert, and another couple traveling with them were in Barbados on holiday,

according to Inspector Mervin Brathwaite of the Royal Barbados Police Force.

Flanked by the force's top brass at a hastily called news conference at Police Headquarters, Roebuck Street, Commissioner Arundel Small stressed that Barbados remains safe for residents and visitors alike.

"The year has barely begun," he said, "but we are confident that our efforts will reduce the rate of violent crimes compared to 2016."

Homicides against tourists are extremely rare in Barbados, Small stressed, noting that in most years there are none. The majority of violent crimes on the island are drug-gang related, he said.

Asked whether police believe the murder of Ms. Coe was the result of a botched robbery, Brathwaite said, "At this point I don't wish to speak about the direction of the investigation, except to say that it will be intensive, thorough, and ultimately successful."

"That doesn't sound like cop-speak," I opined, after reading the paragraph out loud.

"Maybe he ran it through the local constabulary's highly paid communications director," Lynda quipped.

"Do not underestimate Inspector Brathwaite," Mac warned. "In our brief encounter he displayed both imagination and ambition, which can be a powerful combination. Imagination caused him to look beyond the obvious burglary scenario to consider other possibilities, and ambition caused him to accede to Sir Owen's request to humor me although he clearly chafed under it."

The newspaper story went on for another fifteen paragraphs. Right after Brathwaite's first quoted comment, the journalist dutifully reported a representative of the

Aquarius as assuring the hotel's dedication to "the comfort and security of all our guests." Brathwaite, in turn, acknowledged that there was "no evidence of a break-in." The reporter seemed to think that cut in the hotel's favor, but I wasn't buying it.

"If there was no forced entry, it's probably because the intruder was a hotel employee with a key," I said. "How else would a thief get into the room without forcing the lock?"

"Perhaps Ms. Coe let him in," Mac suggested. "I am assuming a 'he' because of the violent nature of the attack, although perhaps I assume too much. Or one could construct another scenario: A thief gained entrance by pretense, intending to snatch and grab valuables, and then was forced to more drastic measures to silence Ms. Coe."

"I like my idea better. A hotel employee would be better positioned to know that Sabrina was rich and likely to have something worth stealing."

"Barbados caters to high-end tourism, T.J.," Kate said. "Wealthy holidaymakers aren't a rarity here, and I'm sure the Aquarius gets its share. I can't see why Sabrina would be a particular target."

"On the other hand, this isn't a common single-destination for Americans," Lynda mused. "They usually come here on a 'If it's Tuesday, this must be Bermuda' cruise. I wonder how Coe and Company wound up here."

"The story mentioned in the twelfth paragraph that the couple's friend Marcus Wagner has what the author vaguely called 'business interests' on the island," Mac pointed out. "Perhaps that was the reason."

"Well, whatever," I said, "it's got to be a nightmare for Mo. How would you like to wake up and find a headline like that"—I pointed—"on your wedding day?"

"At least there will *be* a wedding, old boy," Mac said.

"Speaking of which—" As Lynda said this, she and Kate rose at the same time. "We'd better get dressed and help Mo get ready."

The nuptials went off without a hitch (other than Mo and Jonathan getting hitched) right there at Naniki in the open air amid the lush greenery. Apparently, a lot of weddings take place there. Jonathan and Mac wore white tuxes, matching Mo's very traditional wedding gown. Lynda and Kate wore stunning red dresses in keeping with the St. Valentine's Day date.

The couple not being religious, Sir Owen presided over a civil ceremony under his authority as a marriage officer, which is a thing in Barbados law. But he treated us to a talk about holy matrimony, based on the Cana story in the Bible, that would have passed as a homily in any Catholic wedding I've ever attended. Except that Sir Owen talked about twenty minutes longer than the average priest.

Afterwards, Mac hosted a brunch at The Noble Bachelor, an expensive restaurant with an expansive view of the Caribbean, in lieu of a reception highlighted by "Proud Mary" and the chicken dance. That was okay with me. At no point did Mo toss her garter or her bouquet of red flowers. I ate chilled leek and potato soup with sautéed scallops and truffle oil for the first course, followed by Cajun salmon with pesto cream sauce, creamed potatoes, grilled zucchini, and tomato salsa. Just in case you wondered. I noticed that Lynda chose chargrilled mahi-mahi and Mac tucked into a 12-ounce prime sirloin steak.

"Well, young people, you can hardly say that your wedding has been uneventful," Sir Owen commented as the second course was being brought in.

The smile on Mo's face took a hike. "I'm so happy today"—she slid her freshly-minted husband an adoring look—"and yet I can't stop thinking about Sabrina. I even feel sorry for Art."

Jonathan took her hand. He did that a lot.

"I hope the killer will be brought quickly to justice, my dear," Sir Owen told her. "No, I will do more than hope. I will stay close to the investigation of the case as well as close to you. That should not be so difficult for me." He smiled, showing teeth too imperfect to be false. "I still have friends in high places."

Mac raised an eyebrow. I could guess what he was thinking: Sir Owen told us on our first day in Barbados that he always wanted to solve a real-life murder, just like one of his favorite amateur sleuths. Now he had a chance.

VI

The Caribbean may be laid back, but there was nothing sleepy about the way reporter Jaydene Robinson covered the Sabrina Coe murder. **CYBERSLEUTHS ON CASE** was the headline of her below-the-fold story in *The Nation* on Wednesday. It wasn't your typical second-day murder story. (And I've read plenty!) Here's most of it:

> The murder of an American heiress in her Bathsheba hotel room is attracting attention and theories from amateur sleuths around the world.
>
> Just two days after the strangled body of Sabrina Coe, 37, was found by her partner and traveling companion, the case has drawn hundreds of comments on PublicEye, an internet community of amateur online sleuths with more than 54,000 registered users.
>
> "This case has everything—a violent crime, a rich and lovely victim, and an exotic locale," said Joel Hammersmith, the Washington, D.C.-based owner of the site. "It's murder in Paradise. That's why it went so hot so quickly."
>
> Armchair detectives use PublicEye to exchange theories that range from broad to specific. General concepts put forward in the Sabrina Coe case so far include:
>
> *"The victim was rich. Look at the will!"*
> *"Love or money."*
> *"Drug buy gone awry."*

"Robbery sounds plausible—but locals will cover it up."

More specific theories advanced on the site as to the killer's identity involve individuals mentioned in press accounts of the case.

Several members of the PublicEye community contacted *The Nation* for more information after this newspaper's first story about the murder was picked up by Associated Press and posted online.

"We will investigate any credible leads," said Inspector Mervin Brathwaite of the Royal Barbados Police Force. Asked whether some of the ideas presented on the Internet might have merit, he declined to comment.

The final four paragraphs were mostly a recap of the previous day's story.

"It doesn't mention you or Sir Owen among the amateur sleuths working the case," I pointed out to Mac, handing him back the paper.

"There are amateurs, old boy, and then there are amateurs," Mac informed me.

"Well, I can't exactly argue with that."

We and our spouses were having a Bajan breakfast, including such fare as spicy corned beef and coconut scones. Mo and Jonathan, meanwhile, spent their first morning as a married couple alone. No surprise there! Although Brathwaite hadn't asked Mo to surrender her passport, they promised Sir Owen they wouldn't leave the country.

"Considering that Inspector Brathwaite seems to be getting nowhere with exceptional speed," Lynda said, "I think he could use all the help he can get, no matter how amateur."

"Still, it doesn't take much brain power to figure out that the theories *The Nation* isn't printing because the editors don't want to be sued for libel must involve Russert and the Wagners," Kate said. "I'm sure the police haven't overlooked them either."

"A love triangle!" Lynda said. "Or better yet, a love quadrangle!"

I didn't want to think about the latter too hard.

"Who, then, would be the killer?" Mac asked.

"One of the three who's still alive, of course! You're just playing with me. Okay, I'll lay it out. Sabrina could have been involved with Marcus Wagner. Russert found out and killed her in a rage. The 'hands-on' murder method—sorry!—would fit with that. Or the same scenario of an affair, but Cricket Wagner killed Sabrina to eliminate the competition. Sabrina was a slight woman, so another woman could have strangled her. I think you were wrong to assume a 'he,' Mac."

"That doesn't help clear Mo," Kate pointed out.

"Or maybe," Lynda rolled on, "Wagner 'attempted familiarities,' as they used to say, and she resisted so he killed her."

"Or, since we're not ruling out the females from the suspect list," I said, "maybe Mrs. Wagner is the one who attempted familiarities with Sabrina, and it went south. That could have happened." Not that I had any reason to believe it did. I didn't know these people!

At this point, out of gas, we waited for a response from our resident deductive genius. After a few seconds of silence, Mac raised his hands and clapped softly. "Bravo, Lynda! If Ms. Coe's murder was not the simple robbery that it seems, then it almost certainly was committed by someone she knows. You have done well in laying out several plausible theories."

"But which one is true?" Kate asked.

Mac stroked his beard. "Perhaps none of them. At this point, all I can say is that it is highly unlikely that this murder was fueled by rage, as in your Arthur Russert solution. If the indications of robbery were fabricated to misdirect the police, that speaks of a cool head. One who kills in a fury usually repents and calls the police to confess, departs the scene in a panic, or commits suicide."

"There's always a first time," I said.

"Granted. I said 'unlikely,' not impossible."

"You'd better get on the stick and solve this before Mo winds up in a Bajan hoosegow," Lynda told Mac.

"I don't know what you're worried about," I said. "All those online sleuths are on the case—not to mention Sir Owen Cumberbatch, who is thrilled to be playing Miss Marple."

Pointedly ignoring the dig, but not the unspoken challenge, Mac consulted his Sherlock Holmes wristwatch. "Sir Owen should be here in approximately five minutes. Perhaps he would like to accompany us to the Aquarius Inn to speak with Mr. Russert and his friends."

VII

"Oh, Mr. Russert!" Mac called out.

Arthur Bancroft Russert—not living up to the priggish moniker today—looked haggard, with bags under his eyes and his thick brown hair askew. He wore casual clothes and a backpack. We caught him walking with his surviving travel companions toward the entrance to the hotel, a rectangular, tropical-looking white building with shutters.

"We just got back from the police station," he said. "Now you! What do you want?"

The "you" this time was Mac, Sir Owen, and me. Lynda and Kate stayed behind to meet up with Jonathan and Mo. I later found out that they indulged themselves in tax-free shopping at the Cave Shepherd department store in downtown Barbados. (I believe this is sometimes called retail therapy.) Before they departed, Sir Owen feebly protested that he should stick with Mo (as per his promise to Brathwaite), but his heart wasn't in it. He let Mac talk him into going with us.

"I realize this is a very difficult time," Mac told Russert.

"You have no idea. I blame myself for what happened to Sabrina."

"Perhaps we can discuss it."

"Why?" Marcus Wagner asked. His tone was belligerent, which went well with his brawny body type. "What's your interest?"

"Only to be sure that the murderer is caught, and that justice done."

Wagner snorted.

"I know you've done that sleuthing bit in Erin," Russert said—grudgingly, if I read his tone right—"but I also know that you're Mo's business partner. You're not exactly an objective observer in this situation."

"No, I am not. I am, however, by all instincts a seeker of truth."

I thought that was laying it on a little thick, but apparently Cricket Wagner bought it. She put a hand on Russert's shoulder, displaying a set of nails expertly polished in a lovely shade of coral. "Maybe it would be good for you to talk about it."

"We talked to that cop."

"This will be different," Mac assured him.

Russert didn't jump on it. But mulling the notion for a while, he finally said, "Okay. I don't want to be an asshole about this. Come to my room." And to his friends: "You, too, of course."

The room was spacious, with a canopied bed and a breathtaking view of the rocky Atlantic coastline. It had a rather nautical feel. Russert perched himself on the edge of the bed. Mac sat in a chair big enough to contain his corpulence. The rest of us stood.

"Why do you blame yourself?" Mac asked.

"I talked Sabrina into coming here. We'd been having some, uh, relationship difficulties and I thought the getaway might help."

"But Barbados was my idea, Art," Marcus Wagner put in. Then, to the rest of us: "I suggested it when he said he wanted to go someplace romantic for a week or so."

Mac raised an eyebrow.

"Ah, yes," Sir Owen said. "You have 'business interests' on the island, according to the press account."

"Yeah. I handle U.S. distribution for one of the smaller rum distilleries here, Kill-Devil. Who the hell are you, by the way?"

The old politico laid out his full moniker, not holding back the "Sir" this time. He had no chance to further self-identify.

"Oh! Sir Owen!" Wagner exclaimed, and stood a little straighter. "Sorry I didn't recognize you."

Sir Owen responded with a smile stolen from Mona Lisa. He knew a suck-up when he met one.

"I will lay our cards on the table," Mac said. The only thing he knows about cards is how to make them disappear. "The police have taken what we believe to be an unwarranted interest in Mo as a suspect in Ms. Coe's murder."

"Is that so?" Russert said. "Maybe it's a case of 'what goes around comes around.' Mo tried to poison Sabrina's mind against me when she came here and talked to her alone on Sunday morning."

"Ms. Coe told you that?"

"No. She wouldn't tell me what Mo said. She didn't have to."

"How did it happen that Ms. Coe was alone at the time of the murder?"

"The rest of us were in a submarine."

Mac cocked an eyebrow.

"The Atlantis submarine is a very popular tourist attraction in Bridgetown, not far from National Heroes Square," Sir Owen explained. "It goes down about a hundred and fifty feet. I always recommend it to visitors."

"Sabrina didn't go with us because she doesn't—didn't—like closed spaces. If there were too many people on an elevator, she'd freak out. I called after we disembarked, to tell her we were going to pick her up for early cocktails and then dinner, but she said she wasn't in the mood." He put his head in his hands and started bawling.

"Any more questions?" Wagner snapped.

"A few," said Mac, unmoved. "Inspector Brathwaite said there was no forced entry, meaning either that the killer had a key or Ms. Coe opened the door for her attacker. Assuming the latter, why do you think she did that?"

"She must have thought it was us coming back. Aside from a few government officials and people connected with her non-profit—and they wouldn't be visiting on a Sunday—Sabrina didn't know anybody else in Barbados. Except my ex! If Mo's in trouble, it's her own fault for being here." *That's a little harsh.* "Of all the places in the world to get married, why did she have to show up here?"

Mac could have answered that question, because I'd told him about Mo's late-night confession to Lynda and me, but he let it pass. "Are you aware that this murder has been the subject of much speculation among online amateur sleuths?"

"We saw the story in the newspaper," Cricket Wagner said. "It's disgusting."

"Indeed. And yet, it is a law of physics that random shots occasionally hit something." *I'm not sure that's a law of physics. Probability, probably.* "For example, one of the would-be detectives raised the money motive, which has to be considered in any homicide where the perpetrator is not obvious. Did you inherit from Ms. Coe?"

"You bastard!" That was Wagner, not Russert.

"It's okay, Marcus." Russert sounded weary. "We've been together a few years, Sabrina and me. I know what people will think. But since I manage her money, I can tell you that her will leaves everything to her non-profit, Enterprising Women. I gave Brathwaite her attorney's name to check that out."

One theory down.

"Money is but one common motive for murder," Sir Owen said. "Love is another." Maybe he'd been reading the speculation at the PublicEye website.

In case that was too subtle for Russert, Mac asked, "How would you describe your relationship with Ms. Coe?"

Russert hesitated. "Rocky, I guess, to be honest. She wasn't very happy with me anymore. Like I said, I hoped that coming here for a retreat from the world we knew would change things, but it didn't seem to matter. And Mo didn't help a damned bit!" *Maybe not, Art, but I don't think taking another couple along on a romance-saving vacation was the brightest idea.* "I'm not sure we'd have stayed together, Sabrina and me. But I wish I had the chance to keep trying."

Cricket Wagner handed him a handkerchief and he gave it a workout.

"What about you, Mr. Wagner?" Mac asked.

"What the hell about me?"

"How was your relationship with Ms. Coe?"

"I loved her."

If I'd been sitting, I'd have fallen off my chair. Mac raised both eyebrows. Sir Owen's wise old eyes, which had seen so much in his eighty-plus years, widened. But Cricket looked serene.

"Sabrina was my first cousin," Wagner added, "but more like a sister. We grew up together. I introduced her to Art."

"We were fraternity brothers at Miami of Ohio, Marcus and me," Russert tossed in.

Time to move on.

"Does your business here with the rum distillery have anything to do with the money Sabrina inherited, Mr. Wagner?"

"It has everything to do with it. My dad and Sabrina's dad worked together in Wagner Distributing Co., the family business. I joined the company in the marketing department right out of college. Sabrina worked briefly on the finance side. When Aunt Ruth and Uncle Ray died in a car crash, she inherited their share and sold it back to my dad. She wanted to do her own thing at that point. She used the money to launch her non-profit."

Talking about his family seemed to calm him down. That was a good thing, because I didn't want to get punched by a guy his size.

"Are all of you certain that Ms. Coe knew no one else in Barbados who might have called on her the day of her death?"

"I'm certain," Russert affirmed.

But Cousin Marcus threw in a caveat. "Assuming she didn't meet anybody while she was out by herself on Saturday afternoon."

Sir Owen jumped on it. "Out where?"

"She didn't say," Russert said. "We had a bit of a tiff about something stupid—I don't even remember what—and she hopped in the rental car. She was gone for a few hours in the late afternoon."

"And you have no idea where she went or what she did?" Mac asked.

"No. She didn't offer, and I didn't want to risk asking. I was walking on eggshells because of our argument. She probably spent the afternoon taking pictures with her camera."

"Those are pictures I would like to see," Sir Owen said. "They might be very enlightening for our investigation."

"I share your interest," Mac assured him. "How unfortunate the camera was among the items stolen from Ms. Coe."

VIII

Sir Owen's eyes fairly sparkled with excitement at that. "Remember *Rear Window*, Mac? The reference to a camera reminds me."

The expression on Mac's hirsute face said the question was lame, but he was too polite to make a point of it. Instead, he volleyed back with, "Who could ever forget that Hitchcock classic?"

"Some old movie? I never even heard of it." Cricket Wagner sounded a little impatient. Up to now she'd been a calming influence on her husband, but maybe he was rubbing off on her. "But what does it have to do with anything?"

"Perhaps a great deal, or perhaps nothing." *Feel better now, Cricket?* "I presume Sir Owen has found inspiration in the central plot engine of the film. James Stewart plays a photographer, confined to his Greenwich Village apartment by a broken leg, who becomes fascinated with what he sees in the windows of a neighboring building. He ultimately becomes convinced that a resident there, quite convincingly portrayed by Raymond Burr, has murdered his wife."

"And?" Marcus Wagner prodded.

Sir Owen spoke softly for a man who carried such a big stick, being the ex-Governor-General. "Ms. Coe was a keen photographer, like the James Stewart character in the film. It is only a notion, of course, but perhaps she—knowingly or not—saw and photographed something that posed a grave danger to another person."

If he intended that as a bombshell, it didn't even land like a cherry bomb. Russert and the Wagners just stared at him with "What the hell?" expressions.

"Using a free-standing camera instead of a phone would make Sabrina stand out to anybody who might see her while she was taking pictures," I mused. "Why did she do that, by the way—use a camera?"

"She said it was better for panorama shots," Russert said. "She took a lot of those."

I thought: *Barbados serves up spectacular sunsets. How sad that Sabrina Coe will never photograph another.*

"And perhaps the killer murdered Ms. Coe and stole her camera to conceal whatever it was she took a photo of that was dangerous to that person," Sir Owen said, connecting the dots in case his audience didn't.

The distaff side of the Wagner duo didn't roll her eyes the way Lynda does; she just contorted her face, registering disbelief and displeasure. "Pardon me, gentlemen, but I've had enough of this B.S. Poor Sabrina was killed by a burglar who apparently sucked at his job. Why can't you accept the obvious?"

"There is nothing more deceptive than an obvious fact," Mac and Sir Owen said in unison. I've heard that quote before—Sherlock Holmes in "The Boscombe Valley Mystery."

"I would like nothing more than for the death of Sabrina Coe to be the result of a botched burglary, Mrs. Wagner," Mac said. "Indeed, I argued that solution to our skeptical policeman, Inspector Brathwaite. However, the inconvenient truth is that burglars do not knock on doors. Nor is it likely in such a storied hotel as the Aquarius that the staff, who have easy access to the rooms, have a habit of robbing the patrons."

Cricket showed no signs of being persuaded. "I used to work for an insurance company as an adjuster before I founded Porta-Pal. We handled a lot of theft claims, some of them from hotel rooms." Her mouth turned down. "How ironic!"

"How so?"

"I warned Sabrina not to post pictures of our vacation on social media because it's like advertising to the world that your untended home is ripe for the plucking. By the time I left the business, a lot of insurers were rejecting claims from customers whose houses were broken into if they posted vacation photos on Facebook, Twitter, and Instagram. I told Sabrina that. She ignored me and did it anyway. But it wasn't her home that was burglarized, of course. That's the irony."

"I presume you were her friend on social media as well as in real life?"

"Of course."

"May I see her timeline?"

Cricket whipped out her top-of-line iPhone, worked her fingers over it, and handed it to Mac. I peered over his shoulder as he looked at a parade of selfies-in-Paradise— palm trees here, green monkeys there.

"If there's a photo worth killing for in that batch, how would you know it?" I asked Mac. "And if it's already been posted to the immediate world, what's the point of taking the camera?"

"Oh, I doubt that any of these Facebook photos is significant, Jefferson. None dates from the afternoon before her death, when she was off by herself. It is highly likely that she took different photos with her digital camera then, perhaps with the telephoto lens, and that is what the killer was after. However, we cannot rule out the possibility that she took similar pictures on her cell phone at that time, which she did not post. And Inspector Brathwaite has that phone."

Brathwaite, bearded in his den at the District F Station not so far from the Aquarius, regarded us with approximately the same enthusiasm as I greet letters from the IRS.

"Hello, Sir Owen," was the best salutation the refrigerator-sized cop could manage. Mac and me, he ignored. I'll spare you the social chatter that followed, and fast forward to the meat of the meeting. Sir Owen took the lead in asking Brathwaite questions, not reluctantly. He was in full amateur sleuth mode.

"I understand you have Ms. Coe's smartphone," he stated.

"That's correct, sir. In fact, it's right here." He picked up a soon-to-be-superseded Galaxy S7 Edge from his desk.

"And have you thoroughly examined it?"

"Yes, sir, we have. We paid particular attention to her calendar, her phone calls, and her social media account."

"And what did you find?"

Come on! This is like pulling teeth!

"On the first two items, only negative evidence, I suppose you might say. The calendar was empty, not entirely surprising for someone on holiday. And there were no calls, incoming or outgoing. Her Facebook account was a bit more revealing." Was that expression on his face smug satisfaction? Probably. "Ms. Coe recently became Facebook friends with Maureen Russert, her lover's ex-wife, at Mrs. Russert's request. Thereafter, they engaged in pleasantries, culminating with Mrs. Russert asking to meet with Ms. Coe alone. Ms. Coe responded in the affirmative and set a time to meet her on Sunday at the Aquarius. The only thing I find noteworthy is that Ms. Russert failed to inform me about her social media relationship with the deceased."

Maybe it slipped her mind. She probably gets new Facebook friends every day.

"Then you have missed everything of significance," Mac thundered, clearly unable to contain himself any longer. "This Facebook messaging business establishes that Mo did not merely drop by to visit Sabrina Coe unannounced; she made an appointment. Surely if she intended to visit harm upon Ms. Coe, she would have used that same channel of communication to lure her to some place where she could do so unseen, and then erase the evidence of the rendezvous from her own feed and Ms. Coe's. Instead, Mo arranged matters in such a way that Ms. Coe's three traveling companions knew about their meeting, from which Ms. Coe returned unharmed. And then you suggest that she met Ms. Coe later at her hotel room to kill her, a place where she might easily be spotted coming and going?"

Brathwaite thought about that, but not long.

"Perhaps murder was not her original intention. The first meeting did not go to Ms. Russert's satisfaction, so she suggested a second one later that ended fatally."

I wouldn't buy that crap sandwich if it was free.

Mac gave up. "Have you looked at the photo gallery on that phone?"

"No. Why?"

"Sabrina Coe famously took a lot of pictures—many of them on a Canon digital camera, but not all. I have reason to believe the photos on her phone might be significant. May I have a look?"

Brathwaite looked at Sir Owen, who merely said, "Please."

I give Brathwaite credit for not making a production number of it, the exaggerated sigh and all that. He just handed over the gold-colored phone. Mac accessed the gallery. "I am most interested in any photos from Saturday. Here they are!"

A series of pictures showed a rugged but beautiful coastline from a high elevation, with lots of tropical greenery. Several sequential shots showed the sun setting in spectacular style.

"That's Hackleton's Cliff here in St. Joseph, near the border of St. John!" Sir Owen exclaimed. "It's one of the highest points on the island. A thousand feet above sea level.

Legend says it was named after a man who killed himself by riding his horse off the cliff."

Charming.

"Yes, yes, that's Hackleton's without doubt," Brathwaite said. "Nothing unusual that she took photos there. All the tourists love it."

"Then there would have been numerous tourists watching Ms. Coe take these photos, plus whatever additional pictures she shot on her Canon?" Mac asked.

Brathwaite shook his head. "Not last Saturday. Half the island was at the Hazel Carter concert, especially the tourists."

That would include us, Inspector.

Mac put on his round, tortoise shell reading glasses and scrutinized the photos for a good two minutes.

"There is a drone in two of these photos," he announced.

"A drone?" Sir Owen said. "Are you sure."

"It's the right shape," I said, after a quick look. The object shown in the sky over Hackleton's had two equal-size extensions on each side of the body, with propellers on them. The size was hard to tell, depending on how far it was from the camera.

"Perhaps this drone has some import to the case that is not immediately obvious," Mac said.

"I hardly think so," Brathwaite said. "Drones are quite common, even here in the Caribbean. In the police force we use them to monitor for drug smuggling along the coast."

IX

"This is beautiful," Lynda said the next morning as we stood gazing down at the roiling Atlantic from the heights of Hackleton's Cliff. Too high for my tastes. "And romantic."

Tell that to the poor horse who went over the cliff with the suicidal Hackleton, if the legend is true.

"It's the best view of the east coast," Sir Owen opined.

"I'd like to paint it," said Kate, ever the artist.

Mac just looked, probably for clues.

"It's more than a little creepy to think that Sabrina stood right here, not knowing it was her last full day on Earth," Mo said. There was a little catch in her voice. She turned to Jonathan and changed the subject. "It's hard to believe we've only been married two days."

Any response, verbal or physical, from her newly minted husband was short-circuited by the ringing of Mo's phone. She already had the device in her hand, taking pictures for social media (bad idea—that alerts burglars), so it didn't ring long.

"This is Mo. Oh, hello. Yes, of course. But may I ask what this is all about? All right then. As soon as we can get there."

This can't be good news.

Mo disconnected. "That was Inspector Brathwaite." *Not good news at all.* "He wants me to meet him at the police station. He said he has something to show me."

"Do you recognize this, Mrs. Russert?"

Brathwaite held up what I later learned was a Canon EOS-1D X Mark II DSLR, a $5,000-plus camera with a telephoto lens. I'd seen it before.

"That was Sabrina's," Mo said. "She had it around her neck both times I met her."

"Quite so. Constable Broome found it less than an hour ago in the trash container outside your cottage. Did you put it there?"

"What? No! Of course not! Why would I? And how would I even have it to begin with?"

"Perhaps because you stole it to simulate a robbery after you killed your ex-husband's lover."

"That's not true!"

"I know what's going on here," Jonathan said, his voice trembling from anger. "You people are desperate to solve this case because it's getting a lot of attention around the world, and that's bad for tourism. You probably planted that camera."

"I resent that." No trembling there. Brathwaite was cool as a frozen piña colada.

"May I ask why your constable searched for the camera in the vicinity of Mrs. Russert's cottage?" Mac inquired.

"Because I told her to, Mr. McCabe. When not a single item on the list of articles stolen from Ms. Coe turned up in the usual not-too-scrupulous pawn shops, I thought we should look elsewhere. I reasoned that if the killer was not a thief, she would want to get rid of the merchandise as soon as possible." *She!*

"Well done!" Sir Owen praised. "And I'm sure you realize that by similar reasoning, finding the camera at the Naniki cottages virtually exonerates Mr. and Mrs. Hawes, if I may call the newlyweds that."

Brathwaite blinked. "I don't follow that." Only it came out more like the Bajan "I doan follow dat." Apparently, he talked Bajan when surprised.

"Surely anyone who wished to disassociate himself—or herself—from an object would discard it as far away as possible from her own quarters," Mac explained. "Were there any fingerprints?"

"I'm sure you know better than that." Brathwaite had his English back. "It was wiped clean."

"Not a surprise, to be sure. In view of certain theories that have emerged, I am more interested in the photos inside."

"Also wiped clean, you might say. The memory card is missing."

Mac gave an eyebrow a lift. *The plot thickens!*

"And how do you interpret that development?" Sir Owen asked.

"Perhaps the victim took a photo of her killer, causing the killer to remove it before disposing of the camera."

"That explanation does have the virtue of elegant simplicity," Mac allowed.

Jonathan looked like I would look at a *Downton Abbey* marathon—yearning to get out of there ASAP. "I think we've fully cooperated," he said. "Is there anything else we can do for you?"

Brathwaite must have thought: *A confession would be nice.*

But he said: "For now, just remember not to leave the island."

"And I think it's time you contact the U.S. Embassy," Sir Owen advised Mo.

X

An official named Shalimar Burton at the U.S. Embassy to Barbados and the Eastern Caribbean assured Mo of our country's moral and legal support for a fair trial, if necessary. Translation: *Call us; we won't call you. Meanwhile, get a lawyer.*

"I hardly think a solicitor will be necessary," Sir Owen reassured Mo when she reported the results of her phone call to the embassy. "If Inspector Brathwaite had anything resembling evidence, he would have used it to leverage a confession out of you."

"But I have nothing to confess, damn it!"

I didn't blame her for being a mite overwrought.

"Of course not, my dear."

After assuring Mo that he would get her the best solicitor on the island if it came to that—and simultaneously that it wouldn't come to that because he was going to put his mind to the matter and solve the murder himself "just like Ellery Queen"—Sir Owen departed.

Late afternoon found the wedding party on the veranda at Naniki, contemplating our unhappy situation.

"You're the detective—come up with a solution," Kate ordered Mac.

He sighed. "There is no lack of solutions, Kate. Just look at PublicEye. The number of threads devoted to the Coe murders has multiplied almost geometrically. The challenge is to find the solution that is true and the person who is guilty."

"What about Cricket Wagner?" Lynda said. "Maybe she has designs on Russert—there's no accounting for tastes. I didn't dislike her, in our brief encounter, but I'm sure she's the strong-willed type who usually gets what she wants. She's an inventor and a successful entrepreneur, after all."

"And, therefore, possibly a strangler?" I didn't hide my skepticism.

"Cricket is a sturdily-built gal, remember, and Sabrina was on the small side. I think she could have choked the life out of her."

Delightful image, my beloved.

"That is not a possibility to be dismissed out of hand, I grant you," Mac said. "However, there are difficulties. For one thing, we would have to establish that Mrs. Wagner had time alone with Ms. Coe after the others departed for their afternoon excursion in the submarine. That would have been the only opportunity to do the deed. Also, do not forget that even if she had amorous designs on Arthur Russert, she had a spouse of her own who also stood in the way."

"Not necessarily," Lynda retorted. "Some husbands don't stand in the way."

"Yours does," I quipped.

She crinkled her eyebrows in thought, but apparently not about me. "You know, if I wanted to go away on a romantic weekend to save a relationship, I wouldn't take another couple along."

"I had the same thought," I interjected, waggling my eyebrows at Lynda. She ignored me and completed her observation: "Maybe Cricket engineered it that way."

"I wonder what the Wagners would tell us if we spoke to them alone, away from Arthur Russert," Mac mused. "Well, speculation on that point, at least, is unnecessary. Let us find out."

"Thank you for agreeing to speak with us," Mac said.

"That wasn't my idea," Marcus Wagner grumbled.

"Ignore him," his wife advised. "He hasn't been sleeping well."

Guilty conscience?

We were sitting with the Wagners in a circle on the beach behind the West Indies Rum distillery, producer of Malibu coconut rum. Russert was moping back at the hotel, or possibly in a rum shop, the Wagners told us. Tracking them down had been no walk in the park. Mac called Sir Owen who called Inspector Brathwaite who gave him the Wagners' cell phone numbers. Marcus hung up on Mac, but Cricket told us where to find them. Lynda insisted on going with us, while Kate stayed behind and tried to take Mo's mind off potential decorating schemes for a Bajan prison cell. We had to pay for the distillery tour to get access to the beach— a tour that we were not destined to experience. I hated wasting the money, even at the fixed exchange rate of two Bajan dollars to the American buck.

"Let's get this over with," Marcus directed. "You told Cricket on the phone that you're working with the police." *I wouldn't call it that.* "I hope you're here to tell us they caught the son of a bitch who killed Sabrina."

"Would that I were!" Mac said. *That means no.* "No, I just have a few questions. Inspector Brathwaite continues to believe that the apparent burglary attendant to the death of Ms. Coe was mere camouflage for premeditated murder." Brathwaite never quite put that into words, but he didn't need to. "That conviction has merit. Therefore, I am wondering about any connections your cousin had in Barbados."

Marcus was as surprised by the question as I was, if I read his face correctly. "Sabrina and I have both spent a lot of time on the island over the years. Wagner Distributing has been importing Killer-Devil rum to the U.S. since our parents' time. We used to take family trips here. That's what inspired Sabrina to set up her non-profit to help Caribbean women start their own businesses. She later expanded to Latin America."

"Did she face any opposition here? Perhaps from someone who resented her intrusion as an outsider?"

Marcus was shaking his head before the question was finished. "No, not at all, to my knowledge. Sabrina always had a good relationship with the government and local businesses. Investment in underdeveloped countries is always welcome."

I could have told you that. Mac knows nothing about business, even though he co-owns one. I'm not sure he can balance his check book.

"And she was completely out of the family business?" I asked.

"Completely." So, Marcus presumably didn't profit from her death because of some complicated family trust related to Wagner Distributing. Or that's what he wanted us to believe.

"At any rate," Mac said, "I gather this was not a business trip for anyone involved, whether profit or non-profit. Mr. Russert called it a vacation."

"Right. When he said they were going away and asked Cricket and me to come along, I had no idea they were having relationship issues."

Why does everybody have "issues" these days? Why can't they just have problems?

"So, you had no indication that your cousin had formed another attachment?"

"You mean a boyfriend?" He shook his head. "She never gave me a hint of anything like that."

Lynda turned to Cricket Wagner. Cricket's short, yellow hair glistened with saltwater. She wore a beach robe. "You've been quiet."

"I haven't been asked anything."

"Okay, then: Was there a boyfriend?"

"Not that I know of. And I think I'd know." *Not if the gentleman in question was your husband. Heck, cousins marry each other all the time among the rich and the royal.* I made a mental note to mention that to Mac, which I promptly forgot until now.

"What were your relations with Art Russert and Sabrina Coe? Please be honest."

"I loved Sabrina. Art I could do without. He's my husband's friend, really, not so much mine.."

Reading Lynda's mind was no trick. She had to be thinking: *That's exactly what you'd d say if the opposite were true.* Cricket sounded convincing to me, but I've been fooled before.

"It must have been a burglary," Cricket added. "That's the only thing that makes sense. Look, it wasn't anybody she knew in Barbados, it wasn't us, and it wasn't Art. I'm not fond of the man, but I can't imagine him killing Sabrina in cold blood because she was cheating on him— which she wasn't, I'm sure."

"What about hot blood?"

Cricket shrugged. "Who knows what any of us is capable of in the wrong circumstances?"

I thought: *As a suspect, Arthur Bancroft Russert is a closed door with a brick wall behind it.* Mac had pointed out that this murder didn't have the fingerprints (so to speak) of a crime of passion. That tracked with the Wagners' confidence that Sabrina didn't have a boyfriend in the wings. On the other hand, the idea that Art killed her to clear the decks for a new girlfriend was undercut by the fact that he brought her to Barbados with the stated purpose of renewing their romance. Besides, Sabrina told Mo that she was sure he was "faithful as a dog." Having been "the other woman" in Mo's marriage, she should know the signs. Or so Mo believed, anyway.

The Cody brain was still processing all this when Mac addressed the Wagners:

"You two and Mr. Russert left Ms. Coe alone in the hotel room when you went out for the afternoon on Sunday, correct?"

"That's right," Cricket answered for both.

"Did you linger in the room after your husband and Art Russert went for the rental car?" Lynda wanted to know. *So that they can't be sure she was alive when you left her.*

"What the hell's that supposed to mean?" Marcus exploded. But I'm pretty sure he knew.

His wife ignored the outburst. "Marcus and I weren't even in the room. We met Art in the parking lot. He said he'd always wanted to ride in the submarine, that tourist thing, but Sabrina couldn't hack the idea of the enclosed space and she didn't mind if he went without her. That didn't surprise me, given the mood of the campus between those two. So, just the two of us hung out with Art until we came back to the hotel."

"Every minute?" Lynda pressed. "Didn't he even go to the bathroom?" *You've been reading too many of Mac's mysteries, Lyn.*

"No. The only time he wasn't with us is when he walked away for a few minutes to call Sabrina in privacy. We were right there with him when he found her. I'll never forget that." She paused. When she spoke again, it was with difficulty. "I wish I *could* forget. She was like a sister to me, just like she was to Marcus." Another pause, then: "What makes the police think her murder wasn't a burglary gone wrong?"

Mac fired up a cigar, a sure sign that the McCabe brain was in mystery-solving overdrive. "Other than the fact that Inspector Brathwaite is imaginative and ambitious by nature, his suspicions are stoked by the fact that Ms. Coe's camera was recovered with its memory card missing. That must mean something. Do you see the implication?"

"Something on that card, one or more photos, must point to the killer in some way," Marcus said.

And Brathwaite has a candidate.

"That is the inspector's theory *du jour*, yes."

"I don't see why that shoots down the burglar idea," Cricket said. "Maybe Sabrina took the crook's picture while he was attacking her. Simple as that."

"Simplicity is a virtue," Mac allowed, between puffs, "and yet I do not believe that particular simple answer is the right one. This afternoon, Mrs. Wagner, you reiterated a detail that points to another solution. I was a dunce not to see it earlier. I just need to check a fact with Inspector—"

His cell phone blared out "Ride of the Valkyries." Who says ring tones are passé? "Sebastian McCabe here! Oh, hello. What? You astonish me. Very well, then. I will do my best. Tomorrow."

He disconnected.

"Sir Owen Cumberbatch believes that he has solved the murder. He requests that we—all of us—meet him at Hackleston's Cliff at nine o'clock tomorrow morning."

"This is theater of the absurd," Marcus Wagner said, and I gave him points for the expression. "I'm calling Brathwaite."

"That would be futile, I assure you. Owen has already called the Commissioner of Police, Arundel Smith. At his 'request,' Inspector Brathwaite will be joining us at the Cliff."

XI

Art Russert and the Wagners looked about as happy as Inspector Mervin Brathwaite to be taking in the view from Hackleston's Cliff on that bright Friday morning. Which is to say, not at all. ("What a crock," as Marcus put it so delicately.)

In fact, the only ones reveling in this bit of theater were Sir Owen, who saw himself as the hero of a detective story come to life, and Sebastian McCabe, who did that by habit. But the latter steadfastly refused to amplify, even under the influence of Banks beer, on his hint to us the day before that he had a notion of his own about the killer. He said he didn't want to "spoil Sir Owen's day in the literal sun." All I know is that Mac called Brathwaite, had a minute-long conversation that I couldn't hear, and came away from it with a smile poking out of his beard.

"Thank you all for coming," Sir Owen began. *As if we had a choice.* "You all know why we are here, and I will try to make this denouement brief. Cutting to the heart of the matter, then, the central clue to the whole business is something that's not there. You might almost say—" *But don't say it! Please don't say it!* "—it's like the curious incident of the dog that didn't bark in the night-time in the Sherlock Holmes story." *Damn! He said it.*

"What the hell," Russert muttered. But Mo got it. Her eyes widened a little. Brathwaite just looked pained. Maybe he didn't get it, either. Or maybe he did. Hard to tell.

"I refer, of course, to the last photos Sabrina Coe shot with her digital camera. The memory containing them was removed, but their content is not beyond conjecture. We know from Ms. Coe's cell phone that she stood here, on this very spot, taking photos with that phone on Saturday, one week ago tomorrow."

"That doesn't mean she took similar photos with the camera," my sister said. She's a photographer of no small talent herself.

"Quite so, Kate," Mac agreed. "We know, however, that Ms. Coe often did use both her Canon and the camera function of her smartphone at the same time." We had that from the Wagners. "So, it is a plausible scenario that some of the photos on the missing memory card were taken here."

Sir Owen nodded as if Mac had said "lead pipe cinch" rather than "plausible." "Exactly! And her camera had a telephoto lens. What is it most likely that she photographed from this vantage point, without even realizing it? Drug smuggling!"

Not exactly *Rear Window*, but along the same general lines.

"Smuggling!" Kate exclaimed. "You mentioned that our first day on the island. It's a big thing here, isn't it?"

"Regrettably, yes," Brathwaite interjected. "Large quantities of marijuana and cocaine make their way to our shores, adding to what is produced domestically in the case of marijuana. The Drug Squad is kept quite busy, with the help of the Police Marine Unit, the Coast Guard, and the air wing of the Regional Security System. They seize vessels and destroy the drugs, but a lot of it gets through."

This drug talk reminded me of stories I'd read in the *Nation* . . . along with stories about police corruption.

"Wait a minute!" Cricket objected. Up to now both Wagners, unhappy campers that they were, had been giving the rest of us the silent treatment. "Look around. This place is loaded with tourists and all of them are taking pictures. This is one of the most photogenic spots in Barbados. Why wouldn't it be crawling with tourists taking the same pictures on a beautiful evening at sunset?"

Lynda knew. "Hazel! That was the night of the Hazel Carter concert. It rocked the island. That's where most of the tourists were last Saturday. We've already been over that."

"Precisely!" Sir Owen agreed. "And that, no doubt, is the reason the smugglers were active that particular night. I suspect it was an especially big operation."

"Even if your theoretical smugglers saw Sabrina taking her theoretical photographs, how in the world would they know who she was?" I objected. "They couldn't possibly see her face from this distance."

"No, old boy, but a drone could," Mac said mildly.

"Yes, a drone," Sir Owen said. "I see you follow me, Mac. A drone with a camera, probably live video, captured Sabrina Coe in the act. Photos of a photographer, in effect. And I'm sure you recall Inspector Brathwaite noting that even police use drones these days. No doubt that's how he caught on to the danger to their operation."

Eh? What the—

"Inspector Brathwaite is in league with the drug smugglers, aiding them from inside the Royal Barbados Police Force. He must have had a still photograph of Ms. Coe—one that clearly showed her face—made from the video and taken it around to several high-end hotels until he found where she was staying. A hotel wouldn't give out guest information to just anyone, but they would to a police officer of rank. With that information in hand, he went to her room and, shall we say, dealt with the problem. He killed her and took the camera. That is why from the very beginning he pooh-poohed the most obvious explanation that a thief killed Ms. Coe: In a sense, it was true. A thief did kill her—one who only wanted the contents of her camera."

Brathwaite stood there as immobile as one of those Beefeaters at the Tower of London. *A penny for your thoughts, Mervin!*

For that matter, I had no idea what Mac was thinking either. He appeared to be listening with interest.

"But in Mr. Russert's report to the police, he listed the camera among the items stolen," Sir Owen expounded. "That would never do. Brathwaite needed to return the camera so that attention would not be focused on it. And he did it in a way that implicated a person who might be expected to have strong ill-feelings against the dead woman. That was a good move. But removing the memory card, instead of simply erasing the revealing photos, wasn't so smart. That only called attention to the missing photos."

Kate—bless her—broke in before Sir Owen could evoke the old dog-in-the-nighttime trope again. "But if all that's true, why didn't he erase the photos on her cell phone as well? He had control of the phone while it was at his police station."

"Because to erase the photos from the phone of a woman who was known to post quite actively on social media would have aroused suspicion if another policeman looked at the case. Besides, Inspector Brathwaite knew from looking at them that the photos in the phone didn't show the smuggling operation. Fortunately, he didn't realize how much we could deduce simply from the cell-phone photos telling us where Ms. Coe spent Saturday afternoon." *We?* "Well, Inspector?"

My father, not often given to strong language, nevertheless had an expression that probably summed up Brathwaite's state of mind perfectly: *He didn't know whether to shit or wind his watch.*

"I am at a loss," he said finally. The control required to keep himself from blowing a gasket could be heard in every syllable, even the short ones. "I am here, ladies and gentlemen, at the 'request' of the Commissioner of Police. A request from the Commissioner to an inspector, which hardly ever happens, is not a request. There are dozens of inspectors in the Royal Barbados Police Force and only one Commissioner. He is five rungs above me on the organizational chart. I have never even met him. But he called me yesterday. He told me that Sir Owen Cumberbatch believes he has solved the murder of a tourist, and that I should honor his every request as he reveals the solution. I was highly skeptical, but I am hoping for a long career in the force, so I agreed. Never in my wildest thoughts did I expect what happened here today! All Bajans respect you, Sir Owen. You are a great man, but you are—forgive me—an old man. I think your mental cogs have slipped. This theory of yours is like the last chapter of a bad mystery novel."

"I beg to differ," Mac said mildly. "Sir Owen's conjecture is, on the contrary, like the last chapter of a rather *good* mystery novel—but fiction, nonetheless. Astute reader of Golden Age detective stories that he is, Sir Owen has constructed here an exposition scene redolent of Agatha Christie, with the policeman as the unlikely villain. The only problem is, he got it all utterly wrong. Inspector Brathwaite is guilty of nothing, nor was this murder about drug smuggling."[4]

---

[4] But it could have been. In mid-2018, for example, an online Caribbean news outlet carried the headline: "Multi-millionaire Barbados businessman arrested in $3 million drug bust, yacht suspected in drug trafficking."

XII

"But my logic was flawless!" The great man looked more crestfallen than combative.

"Not quite, Sir Owen," Mac said. "It suffers from an internal contradiction. You assume, on the one hand, that Inspector Brathwaite was both smart and subtle. That is the implication of saying that he did not erase Ms. Coe's photos from Hackleton's Cliff on her smartphone because their absence might be noticed. On the other hand, you portray him as a dolt when you say that he removed the memory card from the camera she wore around her neck. That was even more certain to draw attention when he arranged to have that camera found, according to you, to implicate Mo Russert in his crime."

Mac shook his head. "No, none of that happened. In truth, Inspector Brathwaite challenged the obvious conclusion of a burglary gone wrong simply because that is what a good policeman does. And he was right."

If Brathwaite felt chuffed by that endorsement, he didn't show it. But at least he no longer seemed in danger of exploding. "You have your own theory, Mr. McCabe, I'm sure. That question you asked me yesterday—are you finally going to explain what that was about?"

Mac addressed the rest of us: "I called the inspector to confirm something he said earlier—that Sabrina Coe's telephone showed no calls the day she died. He confirmed that fact. And yet, Mr. Russert and Mrs. Wagner both told me and my associates that the former called Ms. Coe that day and spoke to her after their foray in the Atlantis submarine, thereby seemingly establishing that she was alive and well after he left their hotel room. Can you explain that, Mr. Russert?"

Maybe I'm projecting, but I thought his eyes looked a little wild. "There's some mistake."

"Indeed, sir, and you made it. In my conversation with the Wagners yesterday, I learned two other facts of interest. The first was that they met you outside your room on the day of the murder, meaning they never saw Ms. Coe alive that day. Isn't that true, Mrs. Wagner?"

"Yes," she rasped.

"The other fact was that you walked away from them to supposedly make that phone call to your inamorata. While not inconceivable, that would be highly unusual. Current social mores tolerate the use of cell phones to make calls almost everywhere. Indeed, I often wonder how so many people find so much to talk about. As a result, private telephone conversations are nearly a thing of the past. In this case, I submit that you distanced yourself from your friends not to achieve privacy, but to conceal the reality that there was no phone call. Sabrina Coe already lay strangled, a deed that you accomplished with malice aforethought before you met up with the Wagners that day.

"You suggested the submarine voyage knowing full well that your victim would not participate because—as both you and Mrs. Wagner told us—she was claustrophobic. It was all part of an elaborate plan that began with the highly unusual step of inviting another couple on what was presented as a romantic holiday to repair a frayed relationship. The real reason the Wagners were part of this trip was to provide you an alibi."

"That's not true," Russert said, shaking his head. "None of it's true. It's all crap."

"No, it's not," Marcus Wagner said. "You're guilty as sin. I can see it in your face. You can't fool me. I've known you too long, Art."

Before anybody could stop him, Wagner delivered a haymaker to Russert's square jaw, knocking him to the ground. Brathwaite quickly picked Russert up, holding his arms tightly, while Mac and Jonathan restrained Wagner with equal force. Russert spit blood and a tooth. I wondered what dental care was like in Barbados.

"I just don't believe this," Mo said.

Neither did I. "But you said Russert didn't do it," I accused Mac.

"I said no such thing, Jefferson. I merely disputed the notion that he would have killed his romantic partner in a rage as a result of infidelity on her part."

"Then why did he do it, if not for jealousy?" Lynda asked. "Was he the one who wanted out of the relationship?"

Mo doubted it. "Sabrina told me he was 'faithful as a dog,'" she reminded Lynda. "Although, speaking of dogs, I think for him that would fall into the category of old dog, new tricks. But—as I think I said before—Sabrina would probably know if Art were cheating on her, since she saw his technique when he did it to me."

"Care to comment, Mr. Russert?" Mac asked.

He chose to remain silent.

"That is probably wise," Mac said. He pressed on with his explanation: "We shall have to enter more speculative territory at this point, but I believe the motive for this murder was not love but money. True, Ms. Coe's ardor for Mr. Russert seems to have waned. That was so obvious that he was at no pains to conceal it. Indeed, he rather made a point of it before anyone else could. However, Ms. Coe said something quite significant that Mo quoted only part of a moment ago. She said that Arthur Russert was 'faithful as a dog, but still a dog.'

"That could mean many things, of course, but I believe it was an indication that his perfidy lay outside the romantic sphere—that she discovered he was stealing from her. Remember, he was her financial adviser and money manager before he became her lover. To go even further out on a limb, perhaps she suspected, and he knew it—thus provoking his homicidal intent—but she received final confirmation of the thievery only the day before she died. Perhaps that is what drove her here to this spot on the day before her death, to get away from a man she could no longer tolerate. Were there any calls to or from the States on her cell phone that day, Inspector?"

"There was one in late afternoon—from what I believe is called a forensic accounting firm."

Mac nodded in satisfaction. "And after that call, when they were alone, would have followed a confrontation with Arthur Russert that made the fruition of his plan inevitable, if it was not already. Ms. Coe probably forced him to spend the night elsewhere—that is a checkable fact. He would not have killed her that night; the autopsy would have established a time of death discordant with the scenario he had in mind. He would have come back to their hotel room the next day to do the deed."

"If all this is true," Sir Owen said, "what was that business with the camera all about?"

"It was simple to begin with, and then it became complicated when Mr. Russert tried to be clever. What follows is more conjecture, but I believe that I am on solid ground. Mr. Russert reported the camera among the items stolen as part of the burglary scenario simply because it was so identified with Ms. Coe. In fact, he hid her camera, her jewelry, and her laptop somewhere—possibly his backpack—until he could dispose of them in such a manner that they were not likely to be recovered.

"Then Sir Owen mentioned in his presence the film *Rear Window*, from which arose the clever notion that Ms. Coe had photographed a sight that someone would kill to conceal. For Arthur Russert, that theory had the great appeal that it did not point to him. He hit upon the idea of removing the memory card from the camera—thus giving credence to the theory of an incriminating photo that had to be destroyed—and placing the camera where it might be found. He knew that Mo was already under suspicion, so he put it in the trash near her cottage. Did he suggest that you look there, Inspector?"

"Someone did. We received an anonymous call with a very bad attempt at a Bajan accent." After a slight hesitation (was that embarrassment I saw in his face?), Brathwaite added, "But I already had that idea."

"You bastard," Mo said. She addressed Russert, not Brathwaite.

"You can't prove anything," Russert mumbled, his locution somewhat hampered by a possibly broken jaw.

"Physical evidence is somewhat lacking, but the circumstantial indicators are rather strong," Mac said. "At bottom, what do we have: A woman strangled in the hotel room she shared with her financial manager, who an audit will show was stealing money from her. What do you think, Inspector?"

"I think that is enough to arrest him on suspicion of murder."

He informed Russert of his rights in a statement only slightly different from the one I'd heard many times before. When he was finished, Mo offered some advice:

"You might want to call the American embassy, Art. I can give you the phone number."

XIII

We left Barbados the next day, but not before a romantic torchlit supper for six at The Cliff, a famous $$$$ restaurant hanging out over the ocean. Sir Owen, working hard to get over the disappointment of his failed Ellery Queen audition, recommended it.

"Just think," Lynda said, "at this time tomorrow we'll be in Erin with Donata and Polly and Oscar and Popcorn. Back home!"

"And back to work on Monday."

We sighed in tandem.

"I can't wait," I said, meaning it.

"Me neither."

You probably know that Russert was convicted of the murder; his trial attracted a lot of attention at the time. I followed the daily accounts on *NationNews*, the online version of the paper we read in Barbados. The Wagners were important witnesses, and not reluctant ones.

Mac was wrong about one thing—the lack of physical evidence. Russert had squirreled away in his luggage three of Sabrina's necklaces, a pendant, five sets of earrings, and two brooches, apparently expecting to sell them in the United States where the Bajan cops wouldn't be looking. The joke was on him, though: The entire haul, all polished glass, wasn't worth more than a few hundred bucks.

That wouldn't have done Russert much good. The prosecutor, a chap named Desmond Adams, established that Russert was millions of dollars in debt. His money woes started with his investment in the failed restaurant that Mo mentioned, and was compounded by his ineptness as an investor. Figuring that the stock market had no place to go but down after an eight-year bull market, he "sold short" a dozen stocks his broker convinced him were overvalued. This would have netted him a tidy sum if the shares had tanked. But instead of bailing out his losses on the restaurant, the ever-climbing stock market put Russert deeper in debt. Maybe he was just doomed to be a loser, but I think he outsmarted himself by trying to play the shrewd investor. I could have told him to stick with index mutual funds.

Why Russert chose the hands-on method of snuffing out the life of the woman who shared his bed never came to light. Mac suggested that "perhaps he realized that murderers are often traced back to the weapon, and so decided not to use one." Personally, I think the SOB just enjoyed it.

Dead on the Fourth of July

I

"Sunscreen?" I asked.

"In my bag."

"Lawn chairs?"

"In the car."

"The baby?"

Lynda rolled her eyes. "In your arms."

Well, I can't keep track of everything. Besides, the little darling is sleeping.

Fourth of July at the Cody house found us loading up Lynda's lovely yellow Mustang to go watch the first-ever Gamble Bank Heroes of Liberty Parade in downtown Erin. Before long we would have two more kids and a minivan. The new Codys were due at the end of September.

"You know, Lyn, these little excursions are going to get even more complicated when we have a full house."

"At least then *you* can carry the twins once in a while," she snapped, looking down at her sizable baby bump. Said bulge had wreaked temporary havoc on Lynda's spectacularly hourglass figure, and on her mobility. She chugged coffee from her travel mug, the one dose cup of caffeine a day permitted by her doctor. "Can we just get going, Jeff? If we're too late we won't get a good place to sit."

That single tankard of high-test java kept her upright, but it was no remedy for the crankiness of a doubly-pregnant woman who'd stayed up too late to watch holiday fireworks the night before. Having no wish to set off fireworks of our own right there on Campion Lane, I said, "Sure." I also mentioned that she looked smashing in her new straw sun hat and lemon-yellow maternity top, which earned an affectionate response.

Given the series of unfortunate events surrounding Erin's St. Patrick's Day parade the previous year,[5] I was less than enthusiastic about this new town event. But Lynda assured me that Donata Marie, at age 18 months, would be enthralled by the bands and the floats.

Main Street was already crowded at 8:30, but we managed to find an opening on the sidewalk in front of Farleigh & Farleigh, Attorneys-at-Law, for two lawn chairs and a stroller. After getting everything set up, I surveyed our neighbors while Lynda applied sunscreen to herself and Donata. To the right of us sat Louise LaRosa, a well-fed woman whom I knew vaguely as a friend of Lynda's BFF Sr. Mary Margaret "Polly" Malone (Triple M to me). On our left, patriotically decked out in a red-white-and-blue T-shirt, was a man in his mid-thirties wearing one of those shapeless cotton hats that must have a name (though I don't know what it is). While I was almost certain I'd never seen him before, the fellow to *his* left seemed somehow familiar. That chap had a moon face and thick horn-rimmed glasses, with bushy gray-brown hair sticking out of the sides of an Erin Eagles baseball cap. He wore shorts like mine, khaki.

"Nice day," I told Mr. Red-White-and-Blue.

"It's going to be hot," he informed me.

"Hot," Donata confirmed.

With the mandatory socializing out of the way, I pulled out my smartphone and caught up with email, Twitter, and Facebook. Lynda, meanwhile, chatted with Louise while playing with Donata. When I had enough of social media, I started taking pictures of my wife and daughter with the

---

[5] See *Erin Go Bloody*, MX Publishing, 2016.

phone. (Does any gadget do as many different things as a smartphone?) The relationship between mother and daughter is obvious in those photos. Both are beautiful, blond, and buoyant females. Lynda is the one with curly hair, an oval face, and a slightly crooked and incredibly cute nose.

While I passed the time in such a pleasant way, the parade began before I knew it. Leading the procession was a float featuring veterans from a depressing number of wars. Some of the oldest looked like they could have been survivors of the Battle of Gettysburg. Some of the youngest looked too young. Then came the Archbishop Bernardin High School band, reminding me of the final scene in *The Music Man*.

The Reverend Fred Sutterlee of the Apostolic Holiness Church of the Holy Spirit, then acting mayor of Erin, rode in an open convertible behind the band. He'd recently declared himself a write-in candidate in the approaching election, hoping to strike off the "acting" from his job title. His appearance was non-political, of course, as was that of his chief rival, florist and City Councilmember Bruce Gordon. Gordy appeared several entries back on a float full of flowers. Socialist mayoral candidate Lani Alvarez was absent from the cavalcade but busy on Twitter, blasting what she alliteratively called a "parade of privilege."

The Public Library of Erin and Sussex County resurrected for its entry a 1950s-era bookmobile with the message *Next Stop: Adventure* painted on the side. At the sight of it, the patriot to the left of me in the floppy hat formed his hands into a megaphone and yelled: "Take your tax increase and shove it." Then he added something unsavory about "the horse you rode in on." His meaning was no mystery. The portion of the county property tax that supports the library was up for a renewal and increase on the November ballot. The library board said cuts in service, and in library jobs, might be necessary without it. Most of the higher levy would go just to maintain service, although an addition to the historic main library building downtown was also included for a touch of glamour and to attract additional support.

The proposed tax increase faced headwinds from a small but active group of taxophobes, which apparently included the gentleman with the big mouth. It had been a particularly contentious year in Erin, what with the ongoing mayoral campaign and a bruising fight over redevelopment of the old Bijou Theatre. Weary of all that, I had tuned out of the tax fray as much as my job as communications director of St. Benignus University would allow.

Lynda turned around and gave Big Mouth a look that would have curdled buttermilk, if it weren't already curdled. "How rude," she said, ostensibly to me but loud enough for the guilty party to hear it.

Right. Boorish comments should be kept on social media, where they belong.

The subject of Lynda's spoken comment and my silent agreement ignored both of us, to my great relief. Because when he'd put up his hands, his T-shirt also rose— and revealed a gun stuck in the waistband of his shorts. That made me a mite uneasy. Sure, millions of people legally carry guns with concealed-carry permits—Sebastian McCabe is one of them. But I didn't know this guy, and he was within spitting (not to mention shooting) distance of my wife and our daughter. So, I stood up, stepped back, and kept an eye on him as the rest of the parade rolled by.

Just about all the local institutions were on display, from big ones like the sponsoring Gamble Bank and St. Hildegarde Health to the local record shop, Vinyl. Our old friend Oscar Hummel, chief of police, and his unflappable assistant, Lt. Col. L. Jack Gibbons, represented the forces of law and order in their cruisers. Oscar's uniform looked freshly pressed. Eb Schonert's fire department added a splash of color (red) and an EMS vehicle made us feel safe in case anybody keeled over from too much excitement. The guy on my left clapped loudly and cheered for the first responders, I'll say that for him.

When Father Joseph Pirelli, the legendary president of St. Benignus, came into view marching with our Lady Dragons basketball team, I sent a tweet and posted a photo on Instagram to fly the flag for SBU. It's what I do. There are no true off days in my line of work.

"Look, Donata, look!" Lynda exclaimed, pointing. "It's Uncle Mac and Cousin Brian!"

Lynda not being particularly mobile because of her delicate condition, I picked up the baby so the latter could see the indicated male relatives. Then I stepped back, keeping both the parade and the pistol-packing patriot in view.

Sebastian McCabe, my brother-in-law and best friend, and his 13-year-old son Brian rode on a simple float—really a flatbed truck borrowed from Brett McGee's dealership. They were representing "A Night at the Music Hall," a fund-raising show for the Lyceum Theater coming up over the weekend, July 7–9. "McCabe the Marvelous, Master of All Mysteries" was dressed in a tuxedo, thus strongly resembling a particularly rotund penguin with a beard while trying to look dramatic and mysterious. Brian, a budding ventriloquist, held up his "figure" (vent-speak for dummy), an Irish setter named Murphy. The truck didn't have room for the whole cast of the show, but a juggler and a plate-spinner held forth bravely considering that they were performing on a moving stage. Posters for "A Night at the Music Hall," designed by my sister Kate (AKA Mrs. McCabe), had been all over Erin for months.

"Let's wave," I suggested, gamely moving Donata's arms up and down for her uncle and cousin. After not much of that, just until the Lyceum float passed out of our eye-range, I put her down. That's when I noticed the floppy hat on the ground next to my formally vocal neighbor. I quickly glanced his way and saw that he was slumped over in his chair. And I didn't think he was just taking a nap.

"Something's wrong," I told Lynda. I knelt and put my fingers on the unconscious man's right wrist.

"What?" She sprang from the lawn chair with more speed than I would have expected in her condition.

In our excitement, we weren't speaking softly. The guy on the other side of my patient jerked his head our way. He wore sunglasses now, so I couldn't say whether he looked alarmed, puzzled, or curious. Or maybe something else.

"I don't know what," I said, "but his pulse is racing."

"I'm calling 9-1-1."

The response was rapid. I found out later that the EMS vehicle which quickly appeared was the same one that had passed as part of the parade just a few minutes earlier. Floats and marchers parted like the Red Sea to make room for the driver to pull up to the curb in front of us. By this time fingers were pointing in our direction from all over the street, telling the medical types where to go.

Several white-uniformed individuals emerged from the vehicle. A blond-haired guy with a stethoscope around his neck took the lead.

"What happened here?" he asked in a matter-of-fact voice. The voice of experience, I figured.

"He went unconscious," I said. "I was looking at him just seconds before." *Because I was afraid he might shoot somebody.* "I checked his pulse and it was fast. Real fast."

"Is he a diabetic? Sometimes they faint."

I shook my head. "No clue."

"What's his name?" Later, I realized that it's SOP to call patients by name when trying to rouse them.

"We don't know him," Lynda volunteered.

The man in white apparently noticed the face beneath the broad-brimmed sun hat for the first time. "Lynda!"

"Hello, Carter."

Carter Hastings was a name Lynda had mentioned as a fellow student of taekwondo. I must have encountered him in passing at some point, but I didn't recall.

"Wait a minute," Hastings said. "I know this guy—Sally Lobring's husband, Gary. He's met her at class a few times, remember?" Hastings put his stethoscope on the unconscious man's chest as he spoke.

"You're right!" Lynda said. "I didn't recognize him out of context. Sally told me she'd been trying to get him to a doctor. This is awful. Will he be okay?"

"I don't think so." He shook his head. "No, I'm afraid he won't be okay at all."

As the men in white moved Gary Lobring to a stretcher, his gun fell on the ground.

I read in the next day's *Erin Observer & News-Ledger* that he died on the way to St. Hildegarde Health.

II

"Murdered!"

I stared in disbelief at Aneliese "Popcorn" Pokorny, my irreplaceable assistant at SBU and information source without peer. It was Thursday, July 6, two days after the Fourth of July parade that Erin will never forget.

"How could he have been murdered?" I asked.

"Somebody shot him—with insulin."

I wasn't sure which question to ask first, but I settled on:

"How could that kill him? Diabetics do that all the time." I had a high school teacher who shot up with insulin. At least, she *said* it was insulin. She was kind of weird.

Popcorn nodded. "Sure, some Type 2 diabetics do. But if you're not a diabetic, an injection of insulin is fatal."

"I guess that's why he had such a high pulse rate. But wait! When do they figure Lobring got injected?"

"It must have happened during the parade."

"That's impossible! I didn't see anybody get near him, and I would have. I had my steely eyes on him the whole time because he was an angry man with a gun not three feet away from my wife and daughter."

"You must have looked away while you were watching the parade. Oscar looked so handsome."

I considered it—her first statement, that is; the second was delusional—then shook my head. "Uh-uh. I stepped back so I could observe Lobring and watch the parade at the same time. I might have taken my eyes off him for a few seconds, at most, when I was helping Donata wave at Mac and Brian as they passed on their float. But that's all. I just don't believe that anybody could have snuck up on the guy and stuck him with a loaded needle during that short window of time."

"Well, it happened."

Not on my watch.

None of this murder stuff was in that morning's *Observer & News-Ledger*, but I didn't have to ask how Popcorn knew. She and Oscar Hummel are what earlier generations called "keeping company." Both are in their late fifties, equally fond of food and each other. Popcorn, a widowed grandmother, has been trying for some years without much success to make Oscar's mother like her. The Chief is much attached to his mother, though he seems to grow more attached to Popcorn all the time. But I digress.

"I assume the cause of death was determined by an autopsy," I said.

Popcorn nodded her dyed-blond head. "The wife insisted on one."

Ah, the wife. Lynda knew Sally Lobring from taekwondo class, as did the EMS guy. It's a small town, and at times seems even smaller. By all appearances Sally was a successful home-flipper—buying, fixing up, and reselling homes throughout Erin and Sussex County. I'd met her once or twice at events related to Lynda's martial arts hobby.

"I was with Oscar last night when Arly called." Dr. Arlene Eppensteiner was our gung-ho coroner, then still in her first year on the job.

"You guys must have some interesting dates."

Popcorn's green eyes glowed. "You have no idea."

A quick change of subject was in order here.

"I'm just glad SBU isn't involved in this murder," I said. "Still . . ."

"The killer must have been invisible," I told Mac some hours later in his office.

I braced myself for his usual reference to G.K. Chesterton's "The Invisible Man," where the killer is someone that nobody sees because he's such a familiar sight he blends into the background. But it didn't come. Something told me Mac was only half-listening, if that. Maybe that was because, instead of responding, he rolled up his sleeves, making a production number out of showing me his empty hands. Then, in classic magician fashion, he pretended to pull an egg from behind my ear.

"Would you like an omelet, Jefferson?"

"No, I would like you to pay attention instead of practicing for your 'McCabe the Marvelous' gig," I said heavily.

"Very well. My apologies. I doubt that you would care to eat of this particular egg in any case, old boy." He cupped it in his two hands, pressed the hands together, then opened them again. A dove flew out, zig-zagging all over the office. Fortunately, bird crap couldn't do much damage to that room, what with the stacks of papers and books piled up like snow drifts and Mac's bagpipes flopped over a filing cabinet. But why was he messing around with parlor tricks when the big illusion featured on the posters of "A Night at the Music Hall" involved making my sister disappear? I didn't dare ask.

"Now, you were saying?"

"That the killer was invisible. Either that or magic, which amounts to the same thing. How else could the killer have injected a fatal dose of insulin into Gary Lobring while I was watching?"

"Come now, Jefferson! The solution to the apparent conundrum is quite simple, and no invisible men need apply. If the killer did not strike while you were watching, as you insist, then the fatal act must have occurred while you were entranced by the parade and thus had your attention focused in that direction."

"That's what Popcorn says, but I wasn't entranced. And I didn't take my eyes off Lobring for more than a few seconds—not nearly enough time for somebody to attack him."

"Then, as Sherlock Holmes would have said, you saw, but you did not observe."

Since my mother reads these reports, what I replied to that shall go unrecorded.

"There is no alternative, old boy," Mac persisted. "You were a few feet away from the murder scene at the time of the murder. Either you did not see it happen because you looked away at the crucial moment, or you saw but did not realize what you saw. Holmes's favorite maxim still applies after all these years: 'When you have eliminated the impossible . . .'"

"It's impossible that I took my eyes off Lobring long enough for somebody to kill him, I'm telling you. And I didn't see but not observe, either." Then I had a brainstorm: "Hypnotize me!"

A McCabe eyebrow shot up.

"You heard me. Hypnotize me and find out whether I saw something that my conscious mind missed, or if I looked away any longer than a politician keeps a promise. Hypnotizing the witness worked in the *1895* case,[6] and it should do the trick again."

"By thunder, Jefferson, you are right!"

"Don't sound so surprised."

"I can do it right here and now. No time like the present."

Mac turned off the lights, shut the blinds, and lit a candle that he pulled out of a desk drawer.

"Now, Jefferson, the darkness will close in on the light. I want you to focus on the light. Listen only to my voice and to my words. You are relaxed . . ."

"When are you going to begin?"

"I am finished."

---

[6] See *The* 1895 *Murder*, MX Publishing, 2012.

"Eh?"

"You were under hypnosis for fifteen minutes. Would you like to hear? I recorded it all on my phone."

"Maybe later."

I did listen later, and there's no reason to give you a transcript here because it would be repetitive. What I relived for Mac in his office that morning, seeing and hearing the events of the Fourth of July as if they were unfolding in real time, is what I reported earlier in these pages.

"This is indeed a poser," Mac announced. "Based not on your subjective sense but on my own knowledge of the speed at which we progressed along the parade route, and what you saw, I believe that you judged correctly that the amount of time your eyes were off the victim was very brief indeed."

I didn't pause to enjoy this loquacious vindication. "Then what's your explanation of how the murder was done?"

"As of yet, I have none. And the 'how' is not the only enigma. Why kill someone at a public event in broad daylight?" If he had invested more time with that question, maybe Mac would have solved the murder much earlier than he did. "I gather the victim was a controversialist."

"Yeah—apparently he was a big opponent of the increase in the library tax."

Mac cocked an eyebrow. "Motive, perhaps?"

"What, you think Lobring was murdered by an enraged librarian?" I chortled. But later I would rethink that skeptical crack. "I'd say the wife is a better suspect, if it weren't for that fact that Lynda swears she's a sweetheart who obviously loved her husband—even though a lot of other people didn't."

My spouse and I had covered this in a series of texts that morning as I walked across campus to Mac's office at Herbert Hall.

"At any rate," Mac said, "this appears to be no ordinary murder—not the sort that can be solved by routine police work."

Routine, thy name is Jack—Lt. Col. L. Jack Gibbons, Oscar's assistant police chief. Middle-aged and medium in size, he excels in the nuts-and-bolts of police work. At small talk, however, he is not so hot. And he was waiting for me back at the Gamble Building.

We went into my office and closed the door. I don't know why I bothered. Ten minutes after we left, Popcorn would know more about what happened in that room than I did.

"We're talking to anyone who may have seen anything when Mr. Lobring was killed, Jeff," Gibbons explained unnecessarily. "I understand that you were sitting next to the victim all during the parade."

"Right up to the murder. Where did you hear that?"

His lips almost quivered. "I believe Ms. Pokorny mentioned it to the Chief."

Gossip goes both ways!

By this time, I was getting good at telling the story, so I let him have it.

"That's comprehensive and clear," he praised at the end. *Hey, I'm married to a journalist! She works in corporate now, but still* . . . "And you don't think you took your eyes off the deceased for more than a few seconds?"

"I know I didn't. My unconscious says so." Gibbons didn't bat an eye when I explained about Mac going all Svengali with me.

"I see. You said you noticed that Mr. Lobring had a gun. Is that the only reason you watched him so closely?"

Gibbons is such a skilled investigator that I was ready to confess, and I hadn't done anything wrong.

"Not exactly. It was the fact that he had a gun at a family-friendly outing, *plus* the fact that he was a few feet away from my wife and daughter, *plus* the fact that he seemed like a nutball. I mean, he'd just yelled rude comments at the library's float. I know he was some kind of anti-tax crusader, but who in his right mind lobs verbal grenades at the public library—especially at an Independence Day parade?"

Gibbons made a note. It could have said *Cody paranoid* for all I know. "Did you happen to notice who was sitting nearby?"

"Lynda sat to my right." Gibbons knows her as well as he knows me. "Next to her on her right was Sister Polly's friend Louise LaRosa. The guy sitting in a canvas chair to the left of Lobring wore an Eagles cap and sunglasses. Also shorts. His hair was bushy, brown but getting gray. Slightly stocky build. I had a feeling I'd run into him somewhere before."

"That's not unlikely. This isn't Manhattan." *True; we seem to have a higher murder rate.* Gibbons closed his notebook. "Well, this one is a little different. But in the end, it'll probably come down to sex or money. Maybe both."

III

Later that afternoon, Gibbons talked to Lynda—part of what we assumed would be a long process of interviewing anyone on the periphery of the parade who might have seen something. That was unavoidable SOP.

The next day, Friday, the *Observer* led with **MURDER AT THE PARADE**, an account by our friend Johanna Rawls with quotes from Dr. Eppensteiner ("an unusual form of homicide") and Oscar Hummel ("even if you only think you might have seen something, please come forward").

That was opening night for the Lyceum Theater's "A Night at the Music Hall," the gimmick being to recapture the spirit of London, 1895 or so. Since my job at SBU involves touting our faculty as well as the president and official university activities, and since Mac is the entire popular culture department (he's big enough), I naturally tossed out a few tweets and Facebook posts in the days leading up to the performance.

But Lynda and I didn't make it to the show until Sunday, the day that Triple M was available to play with Donata. We double-dated with Popcorn and Oscar in his late father's Oldsmobile. It didn't have a GPS or a rear-view camera, but Oscar had installed the all-import travel mug holder for his caffeine-laced java.

The whole point of music hall is variety, and this show had plenty of that. A Joyful Noise—the tenor trio of a minister (Reverend Mayor Sutterlee), a rabbi, and a priest—sang a medley of patriotic songs. "The Battle Hymn of the Republic" choked me up. Our nephew Brian proved to be an able ventriloquist, but his talking dog had the worst Irish brogue and the lamest jokes ever. (*"What's green and sits in the sun? Paddy O'Furniture."*)

McCabe the Marvelous, Master of All Mysteries, didn't just fool around producing eggs out of some poor schlep's ear. That was only a sidebar. As touted on the poster, the high point of his act was making my sister Kate disappear. He helped her step into a basket, which he then suspended above the stage with the help of a heavily bearded and turbaned assistant. Then he moved on, producing the dove, performing several card tricks, and pulling a stream of American flags out of a previously empty Panama hat borrowed from Oscar. Toward the end of the act, he shot a rifle at the basket. The side of the basket popped down, revealing it to be (*gasp!*) empty. Mac's assistant then removed beard and turban, revealing Kate.

At least, that's what it all looked like to the audience, including me. In the dark of the theater, it was easy to get sucked into the illusion. Magicians can do anything, I mused. *Even kill somebody in full sunlight without being seen.* That thought hit me like a phone call from the IRS. Of course, a stage sorcerer can't really do magic, like Harry Potter or Dr. Strange. But was it possible that the murder of Gary Lobring was a kind of magic trick? Maybe all we needed was a magician with a reason to kill the victim.

Before I could think too much about that, the next act was on—Ralph Pendergast, formerly a daily irritant to me as my boss at SBU and now president of the Sussex County Convention & Visitors Bureau. He capably performed a dramatic recital of the first two and the final paragraphs of the Declaration of Independence. It made me think about why the holiday is formally called Independence Day, which I'm sure was the point. That choked me up a bit, too. Then followed in quick succession a plate spinner, a dancer who was no Michael Jackson, a juggler, a mime, and a comic. The comic should have been a mime and the mime should have been a comic. Names of these performers have been redacted to protect the guilty.

The closing act was another magician, billed as The Great Carlini, who appeared to make a metal ball float in the air and a rope tie itself in knots. He wore a conjuror's top hat, out of which poked a head of bushy hair. When he took the hat off, I saw that on top he was as bald as one of Mac's eggs. I also saw that his right wrist was tattooed with a blue ".

"I know that guy," I whispered to Lynda. "It's Carl Petermann without his glasses." I hadn't recognized him until he showed off his bald dome.

"Shhh."

And then the penny dropped.

The last time I'd seen Petermann had been at the Fourth of July parade, sitting on the other side of the late Gary Lobring. He'd seemed familiar then, but I couldn't place him at the time—either because I didn't know him well, or because I'd never seen him in shorts and a baseball cap.

Peterman was a charter member of the Lyceum Players, the group that performs amateur productions out of the theater. But I'd seen him working as a librarian at the main branch of the Public Library of Erin and Sussex County on Mulberry Street. And yet he hadn't made a peep when Lobring loudly voiced his opinion about the much-needed library tax increase! That was like the dog who did nothing in the night-time, a Sherlock Holmes trope that Mac is forever pulling out. In other words, it was something notable by its absence. Why didn't Petermann push back on Lobring at the parade? *Or did he?*

IV

"And Petermann's a magician!" I told Mac in conclusion that evening.

"Ingenious, Jefferson!" he boomed. That didn't mean he believed my brainstorm—that killing Lobring while I had the taxophobe under close watch was a good assignment for a homicidal prestidigitator. But it was a start.

Kate and Lynda, more like sisters than sisters-in-law in their closeness, were chin-wagging in the living room while Mac and I had a nightcap in his adjacent study. It's where the literary magic happens as the big guy writes his novels and articles. I think of it as his man cave, fully equipped with books on the shelves and beer on tap, but it could just as easily be dubbed Mac's Playhouse. I love the place.

My efforts to get Mac to spill the secret of Kate's disappearance and reappearance having failed, I unloaded on him with my suspicions about The Great Carlini. Mac conceded that Petermann would have reason to be a mite peeved at Lobring for opposing the increase in the library tax. Without the additional funds flowing into the library, Petermann's job might have been one of those at risk. And he was sitting right next to the victim on the parade route!

"However, it does seem unlikely that he would show up at the parade armed with a needle full of insulin, does it not?" Mac asked in a tone of voice that suggested he thought he was making an understatement.

That only stumped me for a few seconds. "Maybe he's a Type 2 diabetic and uses it himself!"

"But have we not established by the rather extreme method of hypnosis that you observed no one, including Carl, get close enough to Gary Lobring to inject him with the fatal substance?"

"Well, yes. But, to my previous point, Petermann is a magician!"

Mac assumed a thoughtful expression as he drew a second beverage from the tap, a craft beer called Flying Pig brewed about forty miles downriver in Cincinnati. "The most important principle in all of stage magic is misdirection, as I have had the occasion to note in some of our previous investigations. Is it possible that, contrary to your recollection, Carl somehow misdirected you, caused you to look the other way and then induced you to forget doing so?"

"No," I said firmly. "That didn't happen. He didn't talk to me and I barely knew he was there. Still—"

"Well, there we are, then!"

And there we were—on the fringes of an impossible crime—until the following Tuesday.

"Mac wants me in his office," I told Popcorn, looking up from the text.

"That means you're in," she said with a look bordering on smugness.

"What do you mean, 'in'? In on what?"

"The Fourth of July Murder, of course." That's the way she said it, capitalizing with her voice. "You didn't really think you and Mac would stay out of it, did you?"

I didn't deign to respond on my way out.

Mac wasn't alone. Sharing his cluttered office was an attractive woman, three or four inches shorter than my six-one, shapely and muscular, with chin length brunette hair. She wore jeans and a T-shirt, as if she were ready to go out and flip a house. She politely rebuffed Mac's attempt to introduce us.

"Jeff and I have met from time to time," Sally Lobring said. "Thanks for trying to help Gary on that awful day."

"I didn't do much," I mumbled. The fact is, I didn't do a damned thing except check his pulse. And then I didn't know what the rapid beating meant. "I'm sorry for your loss."

"Thanks." She didn't linger on that, clearly a down-to-business gal. "I'm here because I don't think the police are doing enough to solve Gary's murder. Lynda said you"—she was talking to Mac—"might be able to help. I should have thought of that myself, you have a track record, but I'm not thinking too clearly these days."

This was an aspect of Lynda's bereavement call on the widow Lobring last night that she hadn't mentioned to me.

"Perhaps you underrate Chief Hummel and his troops, especially Colonel Gibbons," Mac said. "Their many successes receive perhaps a paragraph each in the press while my comparatively few triumphs receive front-page attention simply because they are a departure from the norm." This was McCabe the Modest on display, always a painful sight for me. But what he said was true, of course.

"I'm sure the Erin police are good people, up to the job most of the time, but Gary's murder wouldn't even have been discovered if I hadn't demanded an autopsy."

"I presume you did so because his death was unexpected," Mac said.

"Yes, and no. It was unexpected, but not entirely out of the blue. Gary fainted several times in the last couple of weeks. I kept telling him to go to the doctor and find out if it was stress, arrythmia, low blood pressure, diabetes, or whatever. I found out from Internet research that all of those and more are possible reasons for fainting. Some are life threatening and some aren't, but Gary never took the matter seriously enough to get off his rear end and go to the doctor. I wanted to know what happened to him."

"I don't think Oscar's dogging it," I said. "Gibbons interviewed me, and he's the chief's best officer."

Sally nodded. "I get that, Jeff. All well and good. He interviewed me, too—asked where I was during the murder. I know why he had to ask, but what a waste! Lynda told me you were watching Gary almost the whole time and didn't see anybody get near him."

"That's right." *But Carl Petermann was already near him!*

"Well, I don't know how that can be"—*neither do I!*—"but you would have noticed me if I were there, wouldn't you?"

She was, indeed, very noticeable.

"I'm sure I would have," I agreed. "But just out of curiosity, where *were* you during the parade?"

"Preparing to run the 5K."

I should have known.

Mac raised an eyebrow, which might have meant "*solid alibi*" or "*foolhardy endeavor.*" Maybe both.

"I finished fourth," she added, "but it was a personal best."

"Who had a reason to want your husband dead?" Mac asked.

"To judge by the social media venom, almost anybody who liked paying taxes. Or liked other people paying taxes. Gary belonged to an organization called CATS— Citizens Against Tax and Spend."

"I've heard of that," I offered.

She nodded. "Yeah, well, he was one of the most vocal members, so he drew a lot of fire. The feces really hit the fan when CATS came out against the increase in the library tax, which will be Issue One on the November ballot. The library is very popular, and the part of the county property tax that supports it gets renewed every few years by big margins. I can't say there were death threats when Gary carried the flag for CATS against it this year, but people got heated enough that he never left the house lately without his gun."

"Can you be more specific?" Mac asked. "That is, would you care to name names?"

"Wouldn't that be libel?"

"You're thinking of slander," I said, "but no, it wouldn't. The truth is a complete defense against libel and slander actions in this country. We're not asking you to accuse anybody. Just tell us who your husband had run-ins with."

"Okay. Let's see." I braced for a long list. "A man named Roger Fleming got into Gary's personal space at work and yelled at him about Issue One. Gary felt very intimidated because Fleming's a big, scary-looking guy with an unkempt beard." Big and bearded could also describe Sebastian McCabe, if a hundred pounds overweight counts as big. "He's a high school teacher, but I wouldn't let him teach my kids, if I had any.

"Then there's Jim Bridges, the lawyer who's the chairman of the library board. He used some pretty strong language with Gary during one of the town hall sessions on the issue. From what Gary heard, Bridges was the biggest cheerleader for the idea of hiking the tax—he talked the rest of the board into it."

A high school teacher and a prominent downtown lawyer. We'd encountered more unlikely murderers, though not many.

"Did Gary ever have a row with Carl Petermann?" I asked.

"Who?"

"The guy sitting to his left at the parade when he . . . when it happened. He works at the library."

"The name doesn't sound familiar."

"Can you think of anyone else at odds with your husband?" Mac prodded.

Sally bit her lip. "Just for the sake of completeness, he did have some disagreements with Candace Padget, the chairperson of CATS. She prefers to fight with kid gloves on. That wasn't Gary's style over the last couple of years. He used to say that a polite loser is still a loser." Her eyes misted up. "But he was really a sweetheart beneath all that tough talk. At least, to me he was. I miss him so much. We met in high school and married right out of college."

Mac let that pass for a while in respectful silence until he asked, "Did your husband have any conflicts with other employees where he worked?"

That touched off a memory that made her angry, if I read her facial calisthenics correctly. "Gary used to work at Vinyl, the record shop. But the owner, George Peebles, fired him after that confrontation with Fleming. He called it a 'reduction in force,' but Gary was fired. He wound up working as a Ryde driver for the last few weeks." The smaller competitor to Uber and Lyft had entered the Erin market in a big way just recently with its *Ride with Ryde!* campaign.

"Let me tell you," Sally continued, "rideshare drivers learn a lot about human nature, and it's not good. People show up with alcohol in their hands as if open container laws don't apply in somebody else's car. Or millennials will order up a car to take them to a bar during a blinding thunderstorm as if the laws of nature don't apply for Ryde drivers. And more than once a customer put a very drunk girlfriend into Gary's car and went on partying."

She frowned. "I just remembered something. The night before he died, Gary had a rider who spooked him. He said she brought up the library levy. And then when he responded, she asked him a lot of questions—stuff like why he was so passionate about it, whether he owned a lot of investment property that would be affected by the tax, where the money was coming from to fight it. Gary thought it was a setup of some kind."

Just because you're paranoid doesn't mean . . .

"Did your husband mention this inquisitive customer's name?" Mac asked. "Or say anything else about her?"

"Not that I recall, no. Why would he? If you need the name, I'm sure it's on his smartphone from when she ordered the ride. But the police have that."

"Very well. You have given us four potential suspects. That is a reasonable number of threads, as Sherlock Holmes might say."

"You'll do it, then?" Sally said. "You'll uncover the killer?"

"We can but try, Mrs. Lobring."

"Sally. Thank you. Thank you!"

Apparently not a hugger, she pumped the big guy's hand. Then she pumped mine, too, for good measure.

"I'm familiar with your work fixing up and reselling houses," I told her. I sometimes fantasize about diversifying my investment portfolio with hands-on real estate since I max out on my IRA and 403(b) every year with stock and bond index funds. Property is in my blood. My father is a successful Realtor back in my hometown of Williamsburg, Virginia. "You're an asset to Erin, Sally. You should have your own TV show, like Chip and Joanna Gaines."

"Thanks, Jeff." She had a nice smile. Then she turned sober. "But that would never fly. For one thing, those shows always involve a duo of some sort—a husband and wife, two brothers, a mother-daughter combo, something like that. I'm a solo act in business. Always have been. Gary couldn't hammer a nail into a board without wounding himself. Besides, those shows are all phony baloney manufactured melodrama. Just Google 'home improvement shows fake' and you'll see what I mean. I can't stand fakery. That's what I loved about Gary. He didn't have a phony bone in his body. In fact, he was too honest sometimes, in language that wasn't necessarily the nicest. Maybe that's what got him killed."

V

"I like her style," I told Mac after she'd departed. "There's no BS about her."

"I am inclined to agree, old boy, although I must point out that a successful dissembler *would* seem candid. In a Golden Age detective story, she almost surely would be the murderer."

If only this were a detective story.

"I'll bite. How do you figure that?"

"Because she is the least likely suspect, of course. She qualifies as such for several reasons: Firstly, what could have been passed off as a natural death was discovered to be murder solely because of her efforts. Secondly, she sought out my services. That counts as a mark in her favor, although even Sherlock Holmes was retained by the killer on two occasions."

"You don't really think—"

"No, I do not. In part because, thirdly, hundreds of people must have seen her participating in that 5K race."

In the type of Golden Age detective story to which Mac had referred, meaning the oh-so-clever kind written between the two world wars, that could have been gimmicked somehow. But I didn't go down that hole because I pay some attention to the sport of running. I know that cameras monitor the courses, and computer chips in the runners' bibs track their times at the checkpoints as well as at the finish. These measures aimed at forestalling cheating would also mean Sally Lobring couldn't simply leave the race and pop back in later. And as a runner, she would also know that—or so I assumed.

"What kind of person murders somebody with insulin?" I mused.

"Someone clever and devious."

"Sounds like a job for the Poisoned Pens," I joshed. Our local group of wannabe mystery writers includes a fair share of members who are at least one or the other, clever or devious. Publication has so far eluded most of them. So has success at solving a real-life mystery.[7]

Mac ignored my quip.

"Such a killer also either has free access to insulin, perhaps by theft, or is not penniless. Insulin has become increasingly expensive in recent years, to the point where tragic deaths of those who tried to stretch their supplies have been reported."

How did he know that little tidbit? How does he know any oddball fact? He reads all kinds of stuff, and he could give an elephant memory lessons, that's how. Sebastian McCabe is a font of useless information that sometimes turns out to be useful.

"Our client"—both words were a stretch—"may not think much of the local constabulary," I said, "but I wonder what the Chief is thinking at this point."

Mac checked his watch. "The noon hour is almost upon us. Perhaps Oscar will join us for lunch."

"If you're paying, he'll join us."

"The widow's alibi checks out," Oscar assured us, biting into the heart-attack-on-a-plate known as "The Big Bopper Burger." Daniel's Apothecary, the old-fashioned soda shop next to the *Erin Observer & News-Ledger* offices, is no health food emporium. "The Big Bopper," two quarter-pound cheeseburgers with onions and tomatoes, comes with

---

[7] But they tried in *Bookmarked for Murder* (MX Publishing, 2015).

especially greasy fries on the side. In case that wasn't enough, Oscar ordered onion rings and a chocolate shake to wash it all down. I had a "Sea Hunt" fish sandwich, with Caffeine-Free Diet Coke, hold the fries. You don't want to know what Mac ate. Besides, there isn't room in a novella.

"We didn't really think Sally Lobring was a Black Widow," I told him.

"What? You mean I wasted all that time having Gibbons check her out when I could have just asked your opinion? Next time I'll know better."

Oscar gets waspish when he's hungry. He's often hungry.

"It's not a matter of opinion that she wasn't anywhere near her husband when somebody shoved a needle in him," I said, miffed. "I would have seen her."

"By that logic, nobody did it because you didn't see anybody."

"Touché, Oscar," Mac rumbled. "But enough of this badinage. Please tell us what else you and your officers have done."

Somewhat mollified, he did so. His mood improved as he proceeded through his toxic lunch. "You know we talked to the lawn chair crowd, people watching the parade near Lobring. Jeff and Lynda and Louise LaRosa, for instance. And a guy Gibbons knows named Carl Petermann. Gibbons spotted him in a crowd shot somebody posted on Pinterest. This Petermann was sitting on the other side of the victim, but he says he didn't see anything resembling an attack. He didn't even notice anything was wrong until you started making a fuss over the victim."

"I should have told you about Petermann," I said, mentally thwacking my head. "Carl works for the library, at the main branch. And it's obviously not just a job for him. He's so committed to literature that he has quotation marks tattooed on his wrists."

Oscar frowned and sucked on his chocolate shake. "I hate tattoos."

I ignored this irrelevance. "And yet—get this!—this dedicated librarian didn't say anything when Gary Lobring went into a tirade against the proposed increase in the library tax. Like maybe he didn't want to call attention to himself because he planned to shut Lobring's mouth permanently. And he's a magician, which may explain how he did just that in full view of yours truly without me seeing him. How does all that sound?"

"It sounds like the craziest damned idea I ever heard. Hell's bells! No wonder you gave up writing mysteries, Jeff." He shoveled four ketchup-coated fries into his mouth and worked them over. "As motives go, that one sucks."

"Unfortunately, Oscar, we live in a time of increased tensions and reduced civility in civic matters," Mac said, not eschewing the obvious. "Virtually all issues are highly emotional. In that context, one feels that almost anything can happen. And Mr. Lobring did have a high visibility as an opponent of Issue One."

"If you say so. I guess something like that could lead to a homicide in the heat of the moment, but I don't think that's what we're dealing with here. Unless the killer just happened to have a needle full of insulin with him.

"Anyway, my crack staff is interviewing those of us who were in the parade that afternoon to see if anybody saw anything. Speaking for myself, I got bupkis. I was waving at the crowd and trying not to pop any buttons on my uniform. How about you, Mac? You were on a float."

"I noted Jefferson and Lynda, with my niece Donata in tow. The gentleman next to them was alive and conscious at the time, although apparently he ceased to be mere seconds later."

"With all due respect for police routine," I said, trying to sound respectful, "I don't think this search for somebody who saw something is going to get you anywhere. What about the contents of the dead man's smartphone?"

"Nothing there—no texts to a girlfriend, no suspicious appointments. We gave it a good going over. I'm returning it to the wife with the rest of his effects." "You must have noted that he was a Ryde driver," Mac said. "His interactions with customers were recorded on the phone."

"Yeah. So?"

Mac related Sally Lobring's story of the Ryde patron that Gary thought might be spying on him because of all the questions she asked.

"Opposition research would be the polite name for it," I tossed in. "Remember Lobring's comments about the library tax increase? He wasn't just a guy with a loud mouth and an opinion. He was an activist who might have been seen as a threat to the levy's passage. I can imagine the folks on the other side wanting to get the lowdown on him."

"Okay, I'll give you that, if he was a thorn in their side. But how does that lead to murder?" Burger dispatched, Oscar slurped the last of his shake, making a rude noise. "And if this politically-motivated rideshare customer wanted to kill Lobring—which I don't believe for a nanosecond— why not just do it then and there in his car? Why get complicated about it?"

"Because there's a record of everybody Lobring gave a ride to," I said. "If she killed him while he was on the clock, she might as well sign her name to his body." *Nicely put, Jeff.* "Maybe she was savvy enough to know that."

"Rideshare clients don't kill their drivers," Oscar said inaccurately. "It's the other way around—the rideshare drivers and people posing as rideshare drivers who have killed, raped, and robbed. A very small percentage of them, of course, but it's happened. Anyway, I'm not going to waste any time having my people talk to Lobring's customers, clients, whatever you call 'em. That's a bottomless pit."

Well, that's that. No pesky questions from Erin's finest for the woman Gary Lobring found so suspicious.

"I take it, then, that you would not object if we pursued Mr. Lobring's curious customer"—*The Case of the Curious Customer! Calling Perry Mason!*—"and perhaps talked to one or two other individuals?" Mac asked.

Oscar looked canny. "What other individuals?"

"As I told you on the telephone, Mrs. Lobring does not share my complete confidence in the ability of the Erin Police Department to solve her husband's murder. In response to my request, she identified several persons with whom Gary Lobring was in conflict to a greater or lesser degree. Their names are Roger Fleming, Candace Padget, George Peebles, and James Bridges, the downtown attorney. They all relate in one way or another to the deceased's membership in the anti-tax organization CATS."

"Why am I not surprised? That angle is a bad penny that just keeps turning up. But that dog won't hunt." Oscar stopped, apparently out of clichés. "Go ahead, talk to them all you want. Just don't say I sent you. And good luck. Let me know if you come up with anything. Are you going to eat the rest of your fries?"

VI

On our way back to campus after lunch, we stopped at the fire station for a chat with the last man to see Gary Lobring alive, Carter Hastings of the EMS team.

"I still can't believe they're saying it was murder," were among the first words out of his mouth. "That's just awful. Poor Sally. She must be devasted. He wasn't such a nice guy, but she was sure stuck on him. Anybody could see that."

A little below medium height for a man, and blond-haired, Hastings struck me as the shy, sensitive type—more what you'd expect from a health care professional than a taekwondo practitioner, although he was both. We found him busily washing the EMS truck. He paused at our approach, leaving the vehicle covered in soapy water.

"You knew him well, then?" Mac asked. We were outside, so he lit up a big cigar, an Antonio de la Cova. He smokes less these days than previously but presumably enjoys it more, buying top-of-the-line carcinogens.

"Just well enough to know he was a loudmouth know-it-all with no impulse control, not to speak ill of the dead." *But you are speaking ill of the dead, Carter.* "He came to pick up Sally at the dojo a few times. If you ask me, he should have taken up martial arts to acquire some self-discipline. That's what I did."

He sighed. "Well, Sally's young yet." She was in her mid-thirties, in fact, a couple of years older than I figured Hastings to be. But from where I sit, that's young to be a widow. Not that there's an ideal age for that. "I'm sure she'll get over him in time, find somebody else."

I wouldn't give her the benefit of that old bromide if I were you. Your taekwondo skills might not be up to her reaction.

Mac cleared his throat, maybe to get rid of the taste of that. "Mrs. Lobring has asked us to make inquiries into her husband's death."

Hastings frowned. "You've been mixed up in this kind of thing before, haven't you?"

Are shamrocks green?

"One could say that," Mac acknowledged airily. "Unofficially, of course, albeit not without Chief Hummel's knowledge and even encouragement on occasion. Have the police talked to you about the events of the Fourth of July?"

"Yeah. A young officer." Not Gibbons, then. "He just asked me to verify what was in the written report—that Mr. Lobring died on the way to the hospital."

"No surprise to you, right?" I said.

"What do you mean?"

"You as much as said he wasn't long for this world when you first saw him. How did you know that? He didn't seem so bad to me."

"Experience."

"EMTs must see a lot."

"Actually, I'm a paramedic. I started as an EMT. Paramedics get ten times the training hours. All the more reason I shouldn't have implied he was likely dying. My bad. That was highly unprofessional of me, but I was kind of unnerved when I realized the patient was somebody I knew slightly. That's happened before, of course—inevitable in a town this size. But I've only been in this field three years and I never before had to work on an acquaintance who was dying."

"Most understandable," Mac allowed. "When you arrived at the scene, did you see anyone standing nearby that you might regard with suspicion in retrospect?"

"What do you mean?"

Was anybody carrying a needle dripping insulin? Short of that, I don't know what Mac was looking for. Nor did he enlighten me or Carter Hastings.

"Well, you would know suspicious activity if you saw it," Mac said. "Our dilemma is that neither Jefferson nor anyone else on the scene saw anyone in proximity to the victim—that is to say, in a position to deliver a needle thrust."

"Oh." Hastings looked like a guy trying to look like he was thinking hard. That seemed like overkill to me. "I don't remember anybody like that. But I was busy with the patient."

Mac shrugged that off. "I am not surprised, but it was worth asking. Presumably you also have no special insight as to who would want to kill Mr. Lobring."

Hastings trained a hose on the soap-covered EMS truck and turned on the water. "I hear he was involved in politics. That's a nasty business these days."

"Indeed," Mac agreed. "Indeed, it is."

VII

"So, how was your day?" Lynda asked snuggling up to me on the family-room couch. This cuddling was no easy matter, what with the basketball-sized baby bump, but she managed. Donata was in bed and Lynda had already shared with me the joys of editing her podcast about Sebastian McCabe solving the murder at the Erin opera.[8] This was her current big project for Grier Newspaper Group's North Central Division, parent company of the *Erin Observer & News-Ledger*, while finishing her bourbon-and-horses Kentucky family saga novel at night.

"Oh, you know," I responded, "spin a little, sleuth a little. Just another day in the life of a communications director and dogsbody to a Great Detective."

She hit me with a pillow in the shape of a cat wearing a deerstalker cap. "Come on. Spill."

I did so, giving her a complete account of my adventures with Mac, in chronological order.

"Carter's been paying attention," Lynda said when I finished. "What I mean is, he's right about Sally—and about the hubs, from what I could tell. Sally Lobring is pretty, kind to animals and children, and she could build a house from the ground up if she set her mind to it. You said she pooh-poohed the idea of her own TV show, but she could do it. Gary, on the other hand, was the kind of guy who wasn't always right but was never in doubt. And not even halfway nice about it, in my limited experience of the man. He must

---

[8] See *Death Masque*, MX Publishing, 2018.

have been weaned on sour milk. I never got what Sally saw in him."

"But that's how love is, isn't it, Lyn? After all, what does a beauteous babe like you see in a loser like me?" *A long answer would be fine.*

She wrinkled her brows cutely in thought.

After a while, I got tired of waiting. "Well?"

What happened next is none of your business, but we were good at it even with twins in the way.

"I almost forgot," Lynda said a while later. "You distracted me from telling you what I found out about Gary Lobring."

"Is that what you call it—distracted?"

"As I said earlier," she ploughed on, "I did a little research about him today in my spare time because I thought it might help you and Mac. First, I checked social media. Gary was all over it, a one-man tweetstorm and very active on Pinterest and Facebook. Then I reread all the news accounts in the *Observer* that mentioned him."

"Let me guess: Lobring wasn't shy, diplomatic, or understated about his opinions, including what he thought of anybody who disagreed with him."

"I'll say! He called Jim Bridges, the head of the library board, an 'illiterate moron' during a public forum on Issue One."

"Why? Not that anybody needs a reason to call anybody anything these days."

"Because Bridges defended including graphic novels in the library collection. Gary said people who wanted to look at pictures in comic books should buy them."

"Is that why he opposed the increase in the library tax?"

"Not exactly. That group he's part of, CATS, is against almost any tax on reflex. But Gary pushed out a lot of reasons for voting this one down in particular. The graphic novel stuff was something he threw in along with the kitchen sink. His main contention was that the library is wasting the money it already has by maintaining under-utilized buildings. And to prove it, he posted about ten pictures a day on social media of nearly-deserted rooms in the main and branch libraries."

"That's legit, I guess. Public institutions should be good stewards of public money."

"Fair point. But one of Gary's opponents pointed out that even the busiest businesses are deserted at certain times. The real rub about his photo posts, though, was that in several of them the one or two patrons shown in a big, otherwise-empty library room were minors. Some of their parents weren't happy that their kids' images were used without permission, and they said so. Gary responded by calling the parents things like 'low-IQ idiots.'"

"That's redundant. Anything else?"

"His writing style was a natural for twitter. He would write short messages like 'Don't let the Erin library waste more of your money—vote NO on Issue One' and 'Spend less, don't TAX MORE.' All caps. And if somebody disagreed, he'd hit them with both barrels. 'Elitist' was one of his favorite terms, defined as anybody who supported the library board."

"You mentioned Jim Bridges before. What did he say at that forum? According to Sally Lobring, he had some strong words for her husband."

"Bridges didn't exactly elevate the tone of the debate, either. He called Gary 'an advocate for ignorance' and a 'threat to informed citizenship.'" She made air quotes.

"On the one hand, ouch. On the other, he didn't really take off the gloves."

"Bridges is a gentleman, very old school. You know that. He attacks with long words so that it sounds brainy and sophisticated, but he still attacks."

"What about the guy who really laid into Lobring in his day job? Roger Fleming. Did you run across that name?"

She nodded. "He tweeted that it was a good thing for Gary the Voting Rights Act of 1964 banned literacy tests for voters. I don't think Gary got the insult because he didn't hit back."

This wasn't exactly the normal run of pillow talk at the Cody manse, but highly informative. It reinforced the image of Gary Lobring I already had, although nobody in this ballot box battle was playing nice.

"Lobring was an online bully who brought out the worst in others and inspired more of the same," I summarized.

"Not only online, darling. Don't forget the brouhaha at that town hall meeting. If you need the details, the *Observer* gave a blow-by-blow account. I printed it out for you, along with the other juicy stuff. I didn't pay much attention to that brawl at the time."

"Apparently I didn't either, because I don't remember it."

"The other interesting thing I found in the *Observer* archives was a letter to the editor from Carl Petermann."

"Petermann!" I exclaimed.

"I knew that would catch your attention. Most of it was plain-vanilla stuff, regurgitating the library's talking points: Library revenues from the property tax have gone *down* X percent because of declining property values since the Great Recession. Expenses, meanwhile, have gone *up* X percent even though employees haven't had a raise in five years. The number of items checked out of the library have also gone up over the same period—Petermann gave that percentage, too. He said that shows the library serves the community well."

"You can prove anything with numbers, but that's a good argument."

"Then at the end of the letter, he took a swipe at Gary. He didn't mention his name, but it was obvious who he meant because of his reference to 'strident voices in opposition to Issue One.' He said something like, 'Taxes are the price we pay for a civilized society, but it takes a civilized person to understand that.'"

"That's as gentlemanly a putdown as I've ever heard. Jim Bridges could learn from him. But lots of gentlemen have politely murdered people. Good job of research, my beloved."

I thanked her non-verbally.

"Well, I do have some skills in that area," she said eventually. "Research, I mean."

"You haven't mentioned George Peebles or Candace Padget, the head of CATS."

"Oh, I forgot. Padget wrote an op-ed in the *Observer*. It was a point-by-point takedown of Petermann's letter, longer and more detailed, without getting personal. You can read it later. I copied everything to one computer file for your convenience before I printed it out. You're welcome. You don't really think George Peebles is a suspect, do you—the nice man who sells old records?"

I almost got whiplash from the change of subject.

"Peebles? Not really. Lobring had more reason to kill him than vice versa. I'm sure Lobring resented being fired from Vinyl just because Fleming tore into him while he was working. He probably saw himself as the victim. And Lobring carried a gun, remember."

"There's a lot of that going around."

"Right. It's a scary world and people generally carry with the idea of protecting themselves. That was certainly Lobring's motivation, but how was he to know death was going to come for him in a needle? Which begs the question: Why would somebody going up against an armed target choose insulin as the murder weapon?"

"So it would be written off as a natural death," Lynda said. "And if it hadn't been for Sally demanding an autopsy, it would have."

I ruminated a bit.

"Either that or the killer was a diabetic who struck at Lobring with the weapon at hand," I said. "Or both. But I still don't see how he—or she—did it with me standing there."

"Don't ask me. I'm no good at magic tricks. I still can't figure out how Mac made Kate disappear from that basket and reappear on stage."

"That's easy," I said off-handedly. "She's a twin."

Lynda rolled her eyes. I'm Kate's only sibling. She has red hair like me and stands almost as tall, but is eighteen months older and never lets me forget it.

"I want to meet everybody on Sally's suspect list," I told Lynda. "If one of them was near us at the parade, I'm sure I'll remember. But I know Carl Petermann, AKA 'The Great Carlini,' was there. That, at least, was no illusion."

VIII

Mac added the printout of Lynda's Internet searches to one of the paperwork piles on his office desk, which was somewhat akin to passing water in the ocean.

"So," he summarized, "Roger Fleming, James Bridges, Candace Padget, and Carl Petermann all figure in some quite public and quite bitter exchanges of opinion over the proposed additional library levy. Excellent job by Lynda, by the way!"

"Well, she does have some skills in that area. Research, I mean."

"Indeed, old boy—she is a journalist *par excellence*! Now, I am sure you noticed that most of the *dramatis personae* on Sally Lobring's suspect list were involved in the melee. Even the deceased's mysterious Ryde customer may have hurled some virtual punches, in theory, since her name is not known to us."

"Yet. We'll have that when Sally gets her hands on her husband's smartphone. Since Oscar isn't interested."

Mac nodded his leonine head and returned to his train of thought. "Gary Lobring's former employer, George Peebles, is a notable exception. He seems to have stayed out of the fray."

"Smart dude," I opined. "The owner of a small business in a small town should avoid alienating half his customers, even if he doesn't like their politics. But that doesn't mean he didn't have some unrelated motive for dispatching his former wage-slave. I'd like to cast my baby blues on him and see if he's somebody I remember from the

Fourth of July. First, though, I think a trip to the library is in order."

An eyebrow went up. "You persist in believing my fellow conjuror Carl Petermann to be a good suspect?"

"You saw the swipe he took at Lobring in his op-ed piece?"

"Of course." Mac stuck a hand into the paperwork mess and fished out the printout. ". . . 'but it takes a civilized person to understand that.' Rather nicely phrased, I thought."

"Agreed, but I doubt if Lobring shared our opinion. Maybe he responded outside the pages of the paper, as for example by rearranging Petermann's teeth. And maybe Petermann thought an angry letter to the *Observer* would be an insufficient response."

Suddenly I thought of the Woody Allen movie where he's facing a firing squad and he babbles, "Of course you know this means an angry letter to *The Times!*"

"You are weaving an elaborate garment out of whole cloth, old boy."

"Okay, forget all that," I said, feeling magnanimous. "It's no speculation to say that Lobring was waging a campaign that, if successful, could cost Petermann his job. At least, that was the threat—that the library would have to cut back on staff without the additional funding sought. So that's motive. He also had opportunity—he sat right next to Lobring at the parade."

"Might I remind you that you did as well, old boy?"

I would have ignored that if Mac had given me a chance. But he kept talking:

"And might I also remind you that from your close perspective you did not observe Carl assault the victim?" I opened my mouth. Mac held up his hand. "Yes, I know, he is a magician."

"I was going to say I still find it suspicious that Petermann, sitting right next to Lobring when Lobring unloaded on the library, kept his clever mouth shut. It's like he didn't want to call attention to himself because he had something up his sleeve." *Magician, get it?* "Let's ask him about that. I suddenly feel the urge to get a book from the library."

"I just didn't want get into a fight with a Philistine because I didn't have a slingshot," Petermann explained, if you call that an explanation.

We must have looked unenlightened, because he added, "You know—Goliath, David, the Bible. Work with me here, gentlemen."

"We recognized the reference, of course," Mac said. *Of course.* "First Samuel, Chapter Seventeen." *My favorite chapter.* "The giant Goliath was the champion of the Philistines. Your customary wit and felicity of phrase have not deserted you, Carl. However, I find your answer rather lacking."

Petermann, occupying his usual station behind a curved desk on the balcony level of the Andrew Carnegie-built library on Mulberry Street, managed to look sheepish as he put out his hands in a "so sue me" gesture. The blue " tattooed on his right wrist and the " on his left were fully visible beneath his short-sleeved white shirt. The bushy fringe of hair around his bald pate seemed held in place by his thick glasses. Knowing Mac from the Lyceum Players, he'd expressed no hesitation in talking to us. The library was quiet on that Wednesday afternoon in July.

"The truth is, I don't hear all that well," Petermann said. "And in this case, that didn't bother me. I caught enough of what he was yelling to know that Lobring was spouting nonsense about the library levy, may he rest in peace. So, I just kind of tuned him out and recited Tennyson's 'Ulysses' in my head."

"You knew him?" I asked.

"No. At the time, I just knew that he was a jackass. Now I know he was that CATS guy. When I saw the media accounts of the murder, I recognized his name from the paper and a few times when he popped up on the *Crosscurrents* radio show on WIJC. I tried to take Lobring down a peg or two with a letter to the editor I wrote for the *Observer*, but I'd never seen him in person before the Fourth of July."

"And yet, Gary Lobring was a bit of a burr under your saddle," Mac observed.

"I try not to let ignoramuses like that get to me."

"He apparently got to somebody," I put in.

"Yeah, well, not me. My blood pressure is high enough. I don't need to give it a boost."

"Do you also have diabetes?"

He looked at me as if I'd told a joke in Urdu. "Diabetes? No, thank heavens."

Apparently dismissing me as the class clown, Petermann addressed Mac. "I don't know why you're asking me these questions. I'm sorry the man is dead, odious though he was. I abhor violence. Which reminds me. Did you know that he was carrying a gun at the parade?"

The magic librarian didn't exactly shiver, but it was a near-miss.

"You observed that, did you?" Mac said.

"It didn't take a Sherlock Holmes. I saw it fall out of the waistband of his shorts when the EMS guys put him on the stretcher. That kind of unnerved me. Why would somebody bring a gun to a parade? Unless maybe he planned to use it. You never know. There seems to be a mass shooting about every other week in this country."

"You were watching Mr. Lobring closely, then?"

"Then I was. Not earlier."

"I take it that you did not perceive anything amiss regarding him?" *Somebody sticking a needle in the man, for instance.*

Petermann shook his head. "No. I made it a point not to look in his direction after he yelled at the library float."

"Why weren't you on the float?" I asked.

"Why would I be? It's a small float and the big guns were there—Olivia Crewe, our head librarian, and Jim

Bridges, the chairman of the library board, and a few other members of the executive staff and the board."

Something clicked for me. "You said you'd never seen Lobring before. What about at that open forum where he got into a set-to with Bridges?"

"I heard about that, but I wasn't there."

"Why not?"

"It wasn't required, and I had another meeting to go to that night—the Cincinnati Ring of the International Brotherhood of Magicians."

"You are far more faithful in attendance than I, which is highly admirable," Mac said.

"But you heard about the fireworks at the forum?" I pressed Petermann. Somebody had to stick to the subject.

"Heard about it, read about it, sure. It was a big thing in my little world for a while. There hasn't been such a heated library meeting since somebody wanted Olivia to remove *Gone with the Wind* from the shelves because of its racism. But I'm just as glad I missed the donnybrook. I try to avoid conflict."

"That is not always a possibility," Mac pointed out. "And conflict in this contentious age tends to get very personal. Can you recall anyone in your circle of colleagues, friends, and acquaintances who expressed a wish that Mr. Lobring shed his mortal coil?"

"Like in an episode of *Murdock Mysteries* or something?" He gave that a think, or he pretended to. "I can't remember any remarks along those lines."

"Not even from Roger Fleming?" I prodded.

"The teacher? I know him. He wouldn't make a threat—he'd be more likely to knock the guy down and then pick him up. He's one of those short-fuse guys who regrets it later. But, honestly, you don't think *anybody* would be dumb enough to say something like that in public and then carry it out, do you?"

Mac sighed. "One can hope."

Hope was about all we had as we walked back to campus.

"According to the Centers for Disease Control and Prevention, more than thirty million Americans suffer from diabetes," Mac said. "That exceeds nine percent of the population. However, many of them are controlled with diet and exercise, not insulin shots. Moreover, the universe of those with access to insulin includes not only diabetics, but also doctors, nurses, and even family members who administer shots to others."

"Why are you telling me these fun facts?"

"For future reference, Jefferson, I do not think that asking suspects whether they are diabetic is likely to be a fruitful line of inquiry."

"We can but try," I quipped.

Mac's phone erupted with his subtle ringtone, "Ride of the Valkyries." He answered.

"McCabe here. Good afternoon, Mrs. Lobring. All right, then, Sally. Oh, that is good news indeed! And the name? Thank you. No, I am afraid we have little to report. Be assured, however, that we are vigorously pursuing our inquiries. Yes, we will let you know. I promise. Good-bye."

He returned the phone to his pocket.

"Mrs. Lobring wanted me to know that she just received her husband's phone back from Colonel Gibbons. The deceased's last rideshare customer was named Cynthia Brown."

"Who's that?"

"Who, indeed?"

IX

My own phone rang a few minutes later while we were on the road, if you consider the Indiana Jones theme song a ring. It was Lesley Saylor-Mackie, SBU's executive vice president and provost. If you don't know what that title means, it means she's my boss.

"You might want to batten down the hatches, Jeff," she advised. "I just learned from Father Joe that the trustees are going to discuss an across-the-board tuition increase at their August board meeting."

"That's always a crowd pleaser. Well, at least we have time to work on messaging if they go through with it." Not that any spinmeister could make that sound like good news. The best face on it might be something like *St. Benignus University trustees have approved the first change in tuition for students since* . . .

Saylor-Mackie checked on a couple of other irons she'd put into my fire in recent days, then disconnected. I mention this exchange to show you that a manager with a smartphone doesn't have to be on-site to manage. So, I wasn't really playing hooky that afternoon by tagging along with Sebastian McCabe in the Macmobile, a 1959 Chevy convertible the color of a fire engine and almost as big. We were on our way to see Roger Fleming.

A private pool on a hot afternoon in July is noisy, crowded, and pungent with the smell of chlorine. That's where we found Fleming, for whom the Sunny Daze Swim Club was more than a summer job. He was one of four owners, all of them teachers.

Burley and bearded, topping me by two inches and maybe sixty pounds, Fleming wore ragged shorts and a polo shirt I would have passed up in my shopping at the St. Vincent de Paul thrift store. We spoke with him just outside the club's concession stand.

Mac had called ahead, so Fleming knew we wanted to talk about his confrontation with the late Gary Lobring at Vinyl, the record store where Lobring worked at the time.

"I was embarrassed by the whole thing—still am," he said. "I blew my top. What kind of example is that for a social studies teacher?" He didn't wait for an answer. "But I was frustrated by what happened at that open meeting, public forum, town hall, whatever you want to call it, about the idea of raising the library tax.

"It was a week before the end of the school year and the county commissioners were still on the fence about putting it on the ballot. Apparently, Jim Bridges thought an open meeting on the subject would drum up support for what later became Issue One. It seemed a good idea at the time, as they say. I gave my American Government students extra credit if they attended because I expected to hear a civilized exchange of views, with Jim answering reasonable questions from the public. But what happened that night was anything but civilized. Lobring just hurled a lot of insults at anybody who disagreed with his Neanderthal views."

Isn't that an insult?

"Bridges didn't just take it, according to the press account." I pointed out. "He called Lobring a threat to democracy, or some such."

"Yes, but he was right!"

"So," Mac said, "you confronted the deceased at his place of employment."

Fleming stared straight ahead, maybe watching kids splash in the pool. Or maybe he was watching a flashback in his head, as in a movie. "The day didn't start out that way. I mean, confrontation wasn't on my agenda. I just went in there to try to find a Queen album for my son. He's fifteen, plays guitar, and he's really into vinyl. And Queen. I prefer the Beatles, myself. I stop by every few weeks to see if anything of interest has turned up. George gets new inventory of old records all the time."

Fleming stopped.

"Then?" I prodded.

"You have to realize this was just the day after that so-called forum. I walk into the store and who do I see? Lobring. We were already on a nodding basis from the store, but now I know he's a guy who doesn't care if our library system is forced to cut hours and staff. Do you realize how much that would hurt the kids?"

"And you reacted negatively," Mac understated, ignoring the rhetorical question.

"I told him what I thought of CATS, him, and especially his bush-league attack on Jim Bridges the night before. He told me to stuff it. That was mild language for him, but I was in no mood to hear it. I got up close and screamed in his face. I'm not sure what I said. I may have used the word 'asshole.'" *May have?* "And maybe I also called him something else not so polite, questioning his parentage as well as his intelligence." *Maybe?*

Fleming should have been wearing a pair of those socks Lynda gave me for Father's Day, the ones that say, *"Selective Memory Specialist."*

"Lobring probably objected," I speculated.

"You could say that. He yelled back along the lines you might expect from him. We were like a couple of kids in the school yard, only there was no teacher to break us up until George came back from lunch. At that point, Lobring was the one screaming so George apologized to me. But the truth is, I started it. I'm not proud of myself. On the other hand, I think Lobring was glad I started it."

"Why do you say that?"

"Because the fact that he got under my skin validated him in his own eyes, made him important. In fact, the worst part of what I did was that I gave him more notice than he deserved. He wasn't really that significant in the big picture. He was just a loudmouth with a megaphone. I'm talking about his Twitter feed, especially. Today everybody has a voice that reaches to the ends of the earth, thanks to social media. And all too many people think that means they have something to say—whether they know anything about the subject or not. Never mind the facts, much less civility.

"I stress to my students the incredible potential for doing good and for doing harm that they have right in their hands." He held up a shiny new smartphone by way of illustration. "With great power comes great responsibility."

"The Gospel According to Marvel Comics," I cracked.

"Or the Gospel According to Luke," Mac volleyed back. "Chapter twelve, verse forty-eight: 'Everyone to whom much is given, of him will much be required; and of him to whom men commit much they will demand the more.' Revised Standard Version. Newer translations are more gender-neutral."

Whatever.

"Gary Lobring was fired after his contretemps with you, Mr. Fleming," Mac went on. "That must have given you a degree of satisfaction."

"No way. In fact, when I heard he'd been canned, I went to see George. I took full responsibility for the dust-up and tried to get him to give Lobring his job back."

"That was nice of you," I said insincerely.

"Not entirely. In part, I didn't want him to spread the story around that an intolerant library supporter got him fired for exercising his freedom of speech. I could see him doing that as a way of hurting the levy, and I wanted to head him off at the pass."

"You must play chess."

"Not well." *That makes two of us.*

"Obviously, any efforts on your part to save Mr. Lobring's job proved fruitless," Mac said.

"George insisted it was a reduction in force, not a firing—said he didn't have enough business to justify an employee. But I'm sure Lobring and his wife never believed that." He paused. "Look, I'm sorry that Lobring lost his job and I'm sorrier that he's dead. I'm especially sorry for his wife's loss. She seems like a nice person."

"You know her, then?"

"We have the same hairdresser."

You have a hairdresser? Fleming's dark and wavy curly locks looked like a bird's nest after a hurricane.

"Do you have any idea who might have killed Mr. Lobring?" Mac asked.

Fleming shrugged. "How should I know? I'm no Sebastian McCabe."

Puh-leeze.

"Pretend you are," I suggested.

"All I know is, it wasn't some homicidal supporter of Issue One. As uncivil as we've gotten in this country over political issues—and Gary Lobring was Exhibit A of that—I can't believe that anybody would stoop to violence over a library levy."

"Granted, that does strain credibility," Mac allowed, "particularly given that Mr. Lobring's demise is not likely to advance the library's cause. In fact, one could imagine a sympathy vote going the other way."

"Only if you have a good imagination. I don't think this was a political murder." For a reluctant sleuth, he wasn't shy about offering his thoughts. "My bet is that Lobring pushed somebody too far and that person pushed back with extreme prejudice."

"Somebody like Carl Petermann?" I offered.

"Who?"

"He works at the library. Fiction desk."

"Oh. Tattoos on his wrists? I've seen him. He doesn't look like the violent type."

"He says he isn't. But, then, murder by needle is a pretty antiseptic way to do somebody in."

Before he could respond to that, the lifeguard blew a whistle. "Adult swim!" Neither Mac (thank heavens) nor I was dressed for that.

"Thank you for your help," Mac told Fleming. "Just one more question: Have you ever heard of a woman named Cynthia Brown?"

"I don't think so. Who is she?"

"We were hoping you could tell us."

X

You may be wondering why we hadn't yet found Cynthia Brown to speak for herself. We hadn't got around to looking, other than a few desultory and unprofitable checks for a social media account under that name in our area of the world. Mac wanted to pick the low-hanging fruit first, which is why we headed for the law offices of James Hancock Bridges Jr. on Market Street after leaving poolside.

But we took a detour when Mac saw the sign for "Vinyl" at the corner of Market and Broadway. He swung his oversized ashtray-on-wheels into the parking lot behind the record store.

"In a Beatles mood, are you?" I asked.

He didn't respond "yeah, yeah, yeah." I would have pinched myself if he had.

"Let us get Mr. Peebles's perspective on his former employee."

I'd never been in the store, although I'd walked by it for years. Vinyl wasn't one of those new record shops that have popped up to serve music aficionados who insist that digital music just isn't as rich as vinyl, or as mellow, or whatever they say it isn't. The store was "Est. 1978," according to the fancy gold etching on the front door. From the looks of things, that was the last time the place was dusted. One big room was filled with wooden bins full of used albums. Hand-written signs above directed shoppers to Classic Rock, Spoken Word, Classical, European Rock, Jazz, Blues, '80s Metal, and Country. A customer was flipping through the Classical offerings.

"Help you gents?"

The voice behind the counter belonged to a refugee from Woodstock, with long gray hair, wire-rimmed glasses, and a Rolling Stones T-shirt.

"Mr. Peebles?" Mac inquired.

"The same."

"Sebastian McCabe." He produced his hand, which Peebles gave a workout. Peebles had skinny arms. I gave him my name and my hand as well.

"Gary Lobring," Peebles said. He shook his head sadly. "Damned shame."

"Why do you bring up his name?" Mac asked.

He favored Mac with an "Are you kidding me?" stare. "You've never been in this store before, Professor McCabe, but I've read your name and seen your picture in the *Observer* a hundred times investigating murders and such." *You're low-balling it, George.* "I even saw you expose a murderer live on TV once.[9] So you must be here about poor Gary. That's elementary."

Mac looked pained enough for both of us, but he rallied quickly. Peebles was saving us time by cutting to the chase.

"How long did he work for you?" Mac asked.

"About three years. Parker recommended him." He nodded toward the shop's lone customer, a man in jeans with closely cropped white hair, glasses, and a one- or two-day growth of beard.

"Did you get along?"

"Well enough. I didn't like his politics much, but we didn't talk politics. We talked music. He liked jazz. That's my second favorite, behind classic rock." He paused. "Really, he wasn't such a bad dude, just too up-tight. I kept telling him he needed to chill, mellow-out." If George Peebles were any

---

[9] See *Bookmarked for Murder*, MX Publishing, 2015.

more mellow, he'd be dead. "Where did all of his politicking get him? A visit to the coroner's office."

Mac raised an eyebrow. "You suspect his murder resulted from his civic engagement?"

"The thought does come to mind."

"We understand there was quite an imbroglio with one Roger Fleming here in the store."

"Is that what you call it? I'd call it a fight. I had to separate the two. To be fair to Gary, Roger started it. He told me so."

"Do you suspect that Mr. Fleming—"

"Oh, Lord no. Roger's a good customer."

And therefore innocent? Does not compute.

"Is that why you fired Lobring? Because he had a run-in with a good customer?" I wasn't completely buying the idea that George Peebles and his former employee sang a "Kumbaya" duet in their spare time.

"What? No. Where'd you get that idea?" Before either of us could answer, he amplified. "There just wasn't enough business to justify the expense, even if he worked part-time with no benefits. Look around."

I did so. The only customer in the store—"Parker," Peebles had called him—seemed more interested in our conversation than in the records.

"Roger Fleming told us that he tried to save Mr. Lobring's job," Mac reported. "Is that true?"

"Yeah. He's a nice guy, Roger, and he felt guilty. He shouldn't have. Like I said, the layoff had nothing to do with him getting into it with Gary. I just couldn't afford an employee anymore."

The customer gave up pretending to look at records and walked over to us. Close-up, I could see that despite the white hair he was no older than forty. Maybe he dyed his hair, like Andy Warhol. I wondered if his unshaved phiz reflected laziness, a hurried morning, or a fashion statement. His heavy black glasses strongly resembled binoculars.

"Gary was okay when he wasn't parroting talking points from local talk radio," he announced.

"You knew him well?" Mac asked.

"We graduated from high school together at Bernardin. In fact, I dated Sally before he did. But I haven't seen much of him since George cut him loose, just on the street once in a while."

"And you are?"

"Parker Williams."

"The comic book artist?" I asked.

"Guilty."

Around town, the top cover artist for Paragon Comics flies under the radar. But Sister Mary Margaret Malone tells me that when he shows up at comic cons, cosplaying superhero fanboys and fangirls dressed as the Red Raven, Captain Zero, and the villainous Queen Bee mob the guy. He looked like an ordinary dude, what with his Costco jeans and a red polo shirt, but what he did to earn a buck—lots of bucks, according to Triple M—had to take a lot of imagination. I filed that away.

"Your advocacy for your late friend is admirable," Mac commented. "Do you have any idea who took his life?"

"Ideas? I never stop having ideas. But I don't know anything. If I did, I would tell the police, like any good citizen would."

"Mrs. Lobring asked us to undertake a private investigation, independent of the police but not at cross purposes with them," Mac informed him. "What are your ideas?"

"Nothing spectacular. I'm no"—*don't say it!* — "detective, like Batman or the Martian Manhunter. I just think it must have been somebody cold-blooded and methodical, who planned it out in advance to look like a natural death. It wasn't spur-of-the-moment. The killer had to get the insulin."

"The price of that stuff's gone through the roof," Peebles said.

My face must have looked like a question mark, because he added: "I'm a diabetic."

"It could be the old double-bluff," I told Mac back in his car. "Maybe Peebles brought up his access to insulin to throw us off the track."

He muttered something about "gilding the lily." We were on our way to beard Jim Bridges in his metaphorical den. Not that he had a beard—just a thick gray mustache, matching his combed-back hair.

After a leggy admin led us into his standard-issue lawyer's office, Bridges came from behind a big desk to greet us. He might have been as tall as me but for his slight stoop. I figured him as the kind of guy who waited until he was seventy to collect Social Security, and then kept working. We were nodding acquaintances.

"Hello, gentlemen." Handshakes ensued. Bridges had been around forever and done a turn on every board in town, including the SBU board of trustees, before heading the library board. (Did SBU raise tuition on his watch? I couldn't remember.) So, Mac and I knew him, although we didn't exactly eat grilled hot dogs on his patio. In fact, I was a bit surprised to see he was comfortable enough in his own skin to appear in shirtsleeves during working hours. Not many lawyers do that. But, then, Bridges wasn't just a lawyer. He was a legal legend in our community, the best in the business at civil litigation.

"I have to confess I have no idea why you want to talk to me about Mr. Lobring's murder," he said, after directing us to a couple of comfortable chairs and taking the third for himself. "Oh, I know you've been of some help to Chief Hummel in the past." *Like Simon helped Garfunkle.* "I'm not surprised you're at it again. This isn't some open-and-shut street murder. But why talk to *me?*"

"If I may be blunt," Mac began.

"Please do," Bridges said bluntly.

"In seeking a motive for Gary Lobring's murder, it is hard to avoid noting that up to and including the day of his demise he was an outspoken opponent of Issue One. That issue is important to you and many others, and Mr. Lobring was a threat to it."

Bridges was quiet for a minute. I figured he was working out a lawyerly response in his head.

"Except for that Bijou business,[10] you aren't much of a civic player, are you, Professor McCabe?"

"No, I generally expend my energies in other areas."

He nodded. "Maybe that's not a bad thing. Civic activity has been a big part of my life, and I don't regret it, but I kind of cringe whenever I hear the word 'activist' in the media these days. They make it sound like a profession. For me, it's give-back. Some of those full-time 'activists'—left-wing, right-wing, whatever—should be home taking care of their kids. Where was I?"

I have no idea; believe me.

"Oh, yes. You haven't been involved, Professor, so maybe you don't understand that Gary Lobring was only a threat in his own mind. The Public Library of Erin and Sussex County has gotten every levy it ever sought. The private poll I commissioned shows that will happen again. People love the library, and rightly so. Anybody who followed the politics of the levy would know that such an extreme action as murder to further its passage was so unnecessary as to be absurdity. I think you should look for some other motive."

"Such as?"

He shrugged. "I have no idea. Most likely something of a personal nature—an unhappy wife or girlfriend, perhaps. I didn't know the man, apart from one very public and very

---

[10] See *Death Masque*, MX Publishing, 2018.

unpleasant encounter. If what I experienced that evening was typical, finding people who wanted to kill him shouldn't be a problem."

"What about Candace Padget?" I asked.

"What about her? She's the head of CATS. Lobring was on her team."

"If so, it was perhaps a team in turmoil," Mac said. "It has been suggested to us that she and the deceased were at loggerheads over matters of strategy."

Bridges looked thoughtful. "That wouldn't surprise me. Candace is what people used to call 'a real lady' back when I was young, and dinosaurs ruled the earth. She's smart and tough and committed, but she doesn't hate, demonize, or degrade people who disagree with her. In other words, she's not like Lobring at all. I can see where they might have had their differences."

For the record, his characterization of the woman aligned with the tone of her op-ed piece in the *Observer* that Lynda printed out for me, in which Ms. Padget wrote: "We all love the library, not just supporters of Issue One. But home-owning families who are still struggling to recover from the Great Recession simply cannot afford higher taxes. The library needs to find innovative ways to cut expenses, just like the people who pay the bills—the taxpayers." Even though the article took on Petermann's earlier piece in the *Observer* point by point, she mentioned him only in passing as a "highly-respected librarian."

"You seem to know Ms. Padget rather well," Mac commented.

Bridges chuckled. "We've gone a few rounds from time to time. And she used to be my sister-in-law. My wife is a Padget."

Mac raised an eyebrow.

"Candace was married to my wife's no-good brother for twenty-three years and four children," Bridges amplified.

"He's a jerk, my brother-in-law. He proved that when he divorced Candace for a trophy wife."

"You like her, then."

"Like Candace? That depends on the day, I guess. But I sure respect the hell out of her. She's a worthy opponent." Belatedly, he seemed to realize how said opponent's name had entered the conversation. "You don't really think she had anything to do with the murder, do you? That would be absurd. Kill a man over a difference in political strategy? Preposterous. For her or anybody else. Please tell me you're just plowing the ground to see what turns up."

He didn't pick up the ability to turn a nice phrase like that from musty old legal tomes. He probably read a lot of library books.

"Colorfully put," Mac said. "I must remember that. If you are asking me to state that we have no specific reason for asking about your former sister-in-law, that is indeed the case." He paused. "Going further down a highly speculative line of inquiry, is it possible that Ms. Padget had some other sort of relationship with Gary Lobring?"

If I bet on anything other than the S&P 500, I would say the question took Bridges by surprise.

"Relationship? If you mean what I think you mean, I wouldn't know for sure one way or the other. I don't think Candace would engage in a dalliance with a married man, but I've been fooled on that score before. Besides, I suspect that being an independent CPA, chairman of CATS, and the mother of four kids ranging in age from grade school to college keeps her busy enough without adding romance to the agenda. Oh, and she owns three cats. Does that help?"

Sarcasm will get you nowhere, Jim. I should know.

"Possibly." Mac remained unruffled.

"To be frank, if I knew anything pertinent to the investigation of Lobring's murder—which I don't—I would tell the Erin police, not you. If you have questions about Candace, why don't you ask her?"

"We intend to."

"Tell her I said hi."

"Do you know a woman named Cynthia Brown?" I asked.

"Should I?"

"I find it significant that he did not answer your question about Ms. Brown," Mac ruminated as he drove me back to campus.

"Maybe that was just the lawyer coming out. Or maybe he was just tired of your questions." Sensing that Mac might be in a vulnerable mood, I changed the subject:

"How did you make Kate disappear from that box?" I asked.

"Like Sherlock Holmes and that dreadful chasm at the Reichenbach falls, she was never in it. Or, rather, she was in it only briefly before it was raised above the stage."

"Say what?"

"The magicians Penn & Teller refer to 'the principle of simulation,' which they define as: 'To give the impression that something that hasn't happened, has.' This is often done by the magician simply making a casual comment in passing, which leads the audience to see what the magician wants the audience to see. Believing is seeing, as it were. Like the rest of the audience, you believed that Kate was in the box because I alluded to her being there."

"But how—"

"I have said too much already, old boy."

By this time, Mac had piloted his vehicle to the Gamble Building. After a quick stop at my office there, I would head home.

"Too bad there was no simulation about killing Gary Lobring," I said in a parting shot as I left his car. That shows you how wrong I can be.

XI

"I can usually spot your killer by about the third to last chapter, but *The Devil and Damon Devlin* fooled me completely," Candace Padget gushed to Mac. "It's the best book in the series, and I've read them all. But I still can't believe that Ricardo turned out to be the murderer. He's been in every book since *Hocus-Pocus*."

Maybe I should have asked for caffeinated coffee, never mind that it's toxic.

The morning after our chat with Jim Bridges, and nine days after the Fourth of July murder, we were drinking java out of CATS mugs in the small offices of Candace Ridgely Padget CPA LLC. ("It's my husband's last name, but I'm not giving it up. I wouldn't give him the satisfaction.") She was thirty or forty pounds overweight, but dressed in a caftan to deemphasize the surplus avoirdupois. Her hair was beige, in contrast to her rather colorful personality.

On her desk lay that morning's *Erin Observer & News-Ledger* with the headline **JULY 4 SLAYING ELUDES SOLUTION**. The story, again by Johanna Rawls, was mostly rehash and Oscar saying, "The case remains under active investigation." Neither Sebastian McCabe nor I was mentioned as being involved in the case, which was okay by me but wouldn't elude Johanna (I call her "Tall Rawls") much longer. Crime is her beat. Lower on the page was a feature story about a hobbyist who had found three cheaters in Erin's Fourth of July 5K race by using checkpoint times, course maps, eyewitness accounts, and photos. Sally Lobring, no surprise to me, was not among the miscreants.

"Anyway, I can't wait for your next book," Padget told Mac.

"You are too kind," he said. *I agree.* "If only my acquaintance with murder were limited to literature."

Padget turned sober, blinking her wide black eyes. "I'm still in shock about Gary's death. You said you wanted to talk to me about that. I suppose you want to know who I think would want to kill him."

"We already have a rather long list. He was a controversial figure. Perhaps it would save time to say that we are aware he had rather public confrontations with James Bridges, Carl Petermann, and Roger Fleming. He was let go by his employer shortly after the latter, although the employer denies a cause-and-effect connection."

"Gary was a pain in the ass," the CPA admitted, "even to me—and I was on his side. His wife must be a saint to have put up with him."

Saint, enabler, survivor, Stockholm Syndrome victim—take your pick. Who knew what their marriage was like on the inside? I once saw the prickly misanthrope Bruce Gordon, florist and City Councilmember, practically melt with kindness when he was talking to his cancer-stricken wife on the phone.

"I gather you had strategic differences," Mac said.

"No, we had tactical differences. Gary prided himself on being a fighter. Well and good, but he fought dirty. His bull-in-a-china-shop approach alienated people who should have been our allies. Unfortunately, we're all volunteers at CATS, and you can't fire a volunteer."

Actually, you can. You just have to be willing accept the consequences, which may not be worth it.

"You must be glad to be rid of that problem," I said.

"Gary wasn't a problem; he was an annoyance. People may vote for or against a politician because of his Twitter feed, but I don't think we've yet come to the point

where people will let intemperance on one side or the other
sway their vote on an issue. At least, I hope not."

"Jim Bridges said to say hi, by the way."

She smiled at that.

"We've always gotten along. Jim's old money—
noblesse oblige and very courtly. I was knocked sideways when
I found out he was spying on Gary."

Mac raised two eyebrows. If he'd had one of his
Antonio de la Cova cigars in his mouth, it would have fallen
out. "Would you care to expound upon that?"

"Only if I have your word that you don't say where
this came from."

"Our discretion is absolute, I assure you."

I doubled that.

"A reliable source in Jim's office with a
conscience"—*I bet it was the administrative assistant with the long
legs*—"told me on the QT that Jim hired a retired deputy
sheriff to do opposition research on Gary. A woman named
Cynthia Brown."

Like more than one or two former deputies, Ms.
Brown worked at the Sussex County Courthouse as a bailiff.
We found her there that day between trials, a black woman
in her early fifties, buxom, with long hair dyed with streaks
of yellow.

"Yeah, I called Ryde on July third," she
acknowledged. "It was the night of the fireworks and I'd had
a few brewskis. How did you know? And why do you care?"

Mac ignored the questions. "And the driver was Gary
Lobring, who was murdered the next day."

"Wasn't that terrible?"

"Indeed. You must have been dismayed, given that
you were hired to, shall we say, dig up dirt on the man."

"What? What are you talking about?"

It was the right question, but poorly delivered. She looked more guilty than puzzled, like a fox caught in a henhouse.

"Surely you do not deny asking your driver a multitude of personal questions attendant to Issue One?"

"I might have." She was a terrible liar. "Who remembers what they talk to a Ryde or Uber driver about?"

"Somebody who learned the next day that the driver in question was murdered," I said. It sounded good at the time, at least to me.

"Why are you asking me these questions?"

Mac laid it out: "Mr. Lobring's widow requested us to make some inquiries into his death. The night before he died, he expressed his suspicion that your ridesharing with him was no coincidence. He said you asked many personal questions about how the library levy increase would affect him, as well as how the opposition to the tax was funded. I subsequently learned from a source that Jim Bridges hired you to conduct what is politely called 'opposition research.'"

"Who's Jim Bridges?"

"That, Ms. Brown, is overreaching. No competent person who works in this Courthouse, as you do, could fail to recognize the name of the most prominent civil litigation attorney in the county."

She didn't roll over.

"If he's such a hot shot legal eagle, you don't really think he had anything to do with the murder, do you?"

"All this evasion, on your part and his, makes me begin to wonder."

They kept sparring for another ten or fifteen minutes, but Mac didn't lay a glove on Cynthia Brown. He couldn't get her to acknowledge knowing Bridges—much less working for him on the side. She finally told us she had a job to do and couldn't talk to us anymore.

"I wish you luck, really I do," she said, sounding sincere. "But you're barking up the wrong tree. Even today, nobody gets killed over a ballot issue. I never worked homicide as a cop, but I heard a lot of stories from officers who did. And those stories usually involved money or emotion."

"Gary Lobring didn't seem to have a lot of money," I mused.

Sally, on the other hand, must have done quite well with her house flipping. Not that it mattered to the murder.

On the way back to my office, I returned four urgent emails, six text messages, and two phone calls. Just another day in Paradise.

"You'd better solve the Fourth of July murder soon," Popcorn said as I came through the door. "Oscar's getting impatient."

"Oh, is he? Well, you tell Oscar that if Mac and I are going to do his work for him, we're impatient for a raise."

"A raise? What's that?"

And so forth. She followed me into my office. Mac called me on the office phone in mid-banter.

"Mr. Bridges is on the other line," he announced. "I will patch you in for a conference call."

The next thing I heard was: "T. Jefferson Cody has joined us, Mr. Bridges. You were saying?"

"I was saying, why the hell did you beat up on Cynthia? You terrified the poor woman. You guys are nothing but bullies."

"Wait a minute," I interjected, "I thought you didn't know Ms. Brown."

"I didn't say that. McCabe asked whether I knew her, and I said, 'Should I?'"

"How Jesuitical," Mac said. "As a non-lawyer, I see little difference between your carefully parsed question and a lie. Why did you obfuscate, Mr. Bridges?"

Bridges sighed. We had him. "I didn't want you to drag her into this. That's not fair. A murder investigation, for crap's sake!"

"You dragged her into something unsavory when you asked her to infiltrate the CATS movement."

"Infiltrate? That's not what I asked her to do! Don't be so damned dramatic. I hired her for a little opposition research. Every campaign does that, whether for candidates or issues. I heard around the courthouse that she was looking for a second job to help her daughter who moved back home with two young kids. She worked in Internal Affairs at the Sheriff's Department before she retired, so I figured she'd know something about investigating. You can't possibly think she had anything to do with the murder of Gary Lobring."

Mac didn't, but he sidestepped the question with Jesuitical skill.

"Just yesterday you assured us that Mr. Lobring was an insignificant figure. If that was the case, why did you send Ms. Brown to ask questions clearly designed to establish that he would benefit personally by the failure of Issue One?"

"I didn't. The questions were hers. I told you, she was a seasoned investigator. I just asked her to do opposition research. I didn't even know before the fact that she intended to talk to Lobring. She only told me after he was murdered."

"Your claim that Lobring's death doesn't help your library campaign rings a little hollow," I said. "He may not have been the biggest gun, but he was the loudest."

"Sound and fury signifying nothing, damn you!" Bridges exploded. "No threat at all. I can prove it. Give me your word that you won't share it with anyone, and I'll email you the private poll that shows the vote on Issue One won't even be close."

"Then why pursue this campaign with such vigor that you hired a former law enforcement professional to investigate the opposition?" Mac wondered.

After a pause, Bridges said, "Because I'm tired. I want to spend more time at our house in Florida. I decided earlier this year, along with my wife, that this is going to be my last campaign. I wanted to go out with the biggest possible victory. Wouldn't anybody?"

XII

We made the requisite promise of confidentiality, and Bridges promptly emailed Mac the report from a polling firm, Bohlen & Associates. It showed Issue One cruising to a 71 percent win among likely voters. Bridges' protestations that Lobring was no ballot-box danger seemed credible.

"Where are we going, and why are we in this handbasket?" I asked. I have a T-shirt that says that.

Mac closed his eyes and leaned back in his chair.

"What I mean is," I added, in case he missed my point, "we don't seem to be getting anywhere."

"Do you find any of the individuals we have interviewed to be likely suspects?"

"No."

"Nor do I."

I'd searched my memory banks during each interview, and I was (you should excuse the expression) dead certain that none of the potential suspects had been anywhere near the dead man on the Fourth of July—except, of course, Carl Petermann. And if Mac didn't see a way for Petermann to pull a fast one on me, then it couldn't be done. I was finally ready to admit that.

"Do you find Mrs. Lobring credible in that role?" Mac continued.

"Our client," I reminded him. "Or, she would be, if we had clients. No, I don't find her a believable killer." Nothing we'd heard indicated she was a merry widow. Just the opposite.

"Nor do I. That means we have made great progress, old boy! Even Sherlock Holmes employed the process of elimination in his investigations, and we have eliminated a number of suspects."

Thanks, but I don't need that silk purse any more than I needed the sow's ear.

Mac opened his eyes, relieving my fear that he was going to sleep on me. He assumed a professorial manner.

"Yesterday, Jefferson, you spoke of motive and opportunity with regards to Carl Petermann. Let us revisit that discussion in a broader context, adding means to round out the traditional trilogy of necessities for any homicide.

"First, means—an injection of insulin. There are so many sources for obtaining insulin that 'means' would appear not worth further consideration. I have learned from research that it is not even necessary to obtain a prescription to buy human insulin, and at a much lower cost than the analog insulin that most physicians prescribe today. I assume there is a reason that the analog is preferred for diabetics, but perhaps it is equally fatal if misused. We can explore that later in the unlikely event that it turns out to be germane."

"So 'means' is a dry hole."

"Not entirely, Jefferson. It is worth consideration that, although anyone can get procure insulin, not just anyone would think of using it to kill someone."

Mac had something up his sleeve there. I made a mental note of that.

"We move on to opportunity, which—"

"There wasn't any," I reminded him. "Old Eagle-Eye Cody was watching the victim."

"I was about to say, which eludes us for the moment. That leaves the eternal question of motive."

"Gibbons predicted it will come down to sex or money. Cynthia Brown, on the other hand, said money or emotion. But maybe that boils down to the same thing."

"Or perhaps not. The victim certainly stirred strong emotions that had nothing to do with the heart. Such feelings do lead to murder with depressing frequency, but generally in the heat of the moment except in the case of premeditated hate crimes."

"Well, it wouldn't be too strong to say that a lot of people did hate Gary Lobring."

"And yet, his wife seemed much attached to him."

Mac sat straight up in his chair, not an easy feat for a man of his bulk. "I wonder."

I'll bite. "What do you wonder?"

"Whether it could be that in this case a happy marriage led to murder."

Parker Williams worked out of his house, a mid-century modern split-level in an area of Sussex County that got built-out in the late 1950s and early '60s. His studio on the lower level was decorated with statues of Paragon Comics superheroes (i.e., Captain Zero and the Red Raven) and what I assumed was original cover art of Superman, Batman, Captain America, Iron Man, and Archie by other artists. *Archie?* A mid-century stereo played something on vinyl by the Beach Boys. I felt a keen urge to be back at the Sunny Daze Swim Club.

"I don't know what else I can tell you." Williams, who had shaved since our encounter at Vinyl the day before but still had white hair, seemed exasperated before we even started. "I've already told you more than I know."

"Not quite," Mac riposted. "You are the only person to whom we have spoken who knew Gary Lobring on a deeply personal basis—other than Mrs. Lobring, of course. You mentioned yesterday that you dated her."

"That's ancient history—high school stuff. We were all in the same class at Bernardin High. I took her out a few times in a casual way. I liked her a lot, but she and Gary have been an item since our senior prom."

"Are you still friends with Mrs. Lobring?"

"I guess so. Yeah, sure. Friendly, anyway. She's still the same sweet girl she was in high school. But I only run into her once in a while, always with Gary attached."

Was that a note of defensiveness I detected in his voice? As though maybe he felt the need to explain that he wasn't giving Sally a private exhibition of his . . . drawings? Or was it my imagination? Probably my imagination.

"Did she ever confide in you, as an old friend, that her marriage was in trouble?"

"What? No. That's crazy. You are so barking up the wrong tree. I've been through two divorces and I know what I'm talking about. Those two were joined at the hip. Every time I saw them, they were holding hands. If you think Sally—" He stopped, got a grip. "I know she loved the guy."

This was not the time to tell Williams that could be exactly why she killed him. In theory. I thought that's where Mac was going when he asked—

"Is it possible that the husband she loved so much strayed?"

Williams looked around his studio. "I draw pictures of people who can fly and toss cars over their heads. So, I won't tell you that's impossible. But I will tell you that I wouldn't believe it in a thousand years—for a lot of reasons. For one, he just wouldn't want to. I know him well enough to know that." *You're delusional, Parker. No one even knows what he or she is capable of, much less somebody else. Except me. I'd never do that.* "For another, he was smart enough to know he couldn't do any better than Sally. And if that's not enough, this is a small town. If Gary was fooling around, one of our classmates would have told me."

"Not only do I believe that you believe that," Mac assured him, "I believe that what you believe is in fact the truth." *I think I followed that.* "You have confirmed the testimony of every other person we talked with who knew the Lobrings—their relationship was so strong as to be virtually unbreakable. That could be the key to everything."

"How so?" Williams asked, saving me the trouble.

"Because if someone were enamored of Sally Lobring, the only path forward would have been to remove her loving husband. That being the case, I am almost certain that you were wrong about something else—a false assumption under which I also labored for far too long."

"What's that?"

"You told us yesterday, quite logically, that the murder by insulin of Gary Lobring must have been a premeditated crime. I no longer believe that to be the case. On the contrary, the murderer mistakenly believed he saw an opportunity to have the woman he coveted, and he struck quickly and ruthlessly."

XIII

"Once I discerned the motive, and who might have that motive, the opportunity problem was solved," Mac said in his car later. He'd refused to cough up a name for Williams, but he told me readily enough. It all fit.

"But how are you going to prove it?" I asked. "Where's the evidence?"

"I intend to pursue something better than evidence, old boy—a confession."

He pulled his phone out of his jacket pocket, never mind that I've told him a million times to hang up and drive.

"Who are you calling?"

"Sally Lobring, of course."

Mac began by asking her if she'd been contacted by a certain person since her husband's death.

"Almost every day," I heard her say. "He's been very kind."

Then followed a long talk, which led to arrangements that included us showing up at her home at seven-thirty that evening. It was a three-story Victorian number of the kind known as a Painted Lady, the paint colors being light green, dark green, and cream.

She greeted us at the door, looking anxious. The "us" included Oscar Hummel, who tipped his official hat in her direction. Her brunette hair looked as though she'd been running a hand through it since Mac called.

"I still can't believe it," she said. "I never considered him anything other than a friend. And I'm sure I didn't signal anything else."

"No doubt that is the case," Mac said. "However, your admirer has convinced himself that things will be different with your husband out of the way. Hence, his nearly diurnal phone calls."

"I thought he was just being nice," she repeated. "Are you sure it was something more?"

"We will soon establish that beyond any doubt. Where do you want us to hide?"

This is so hokey. If it doesn't work, I will croak from embarrassment.

"In the dining room. We'll be sitting in the little parlor, which is right off it. I'll close the pocket doors. You don't think he'll get violent when I reject him, do you?"

"I'm armed," Mac and Oscar said at the same time. Sally did not appear comforted. I didn't blame her.

The hardest thing to do in life is nothing at all. The twenty-minute wait after we seated ourselves in the dining room was among the longest of my life. Then the doorbell rang. Sally sprang up to answer it.

"Oh, what lovely flowers," we heard her say.

"I know you like roses. You mentioned that one time."

"Wait for me in the parlor while I put these in a vase." I strongly suspected that she wanted the vase for protection. Feet scurried for a few minutes, then the sounds indicated that both were settled in the parlor.

"How are you?" her guest asked.

"Not great, to tell you the truth. Losing your soulmate is a nightmare you can't wake up from. It's like no other pain you can imagine."

"I know it's hard." Was it just my imagination, or did I hear him moving closer to her on the love seat? "That's why I'm here for you. I'm glad you called me over, like I knew you would. You don't have to go through this alone."

"I appreciate your friendship."

"You must know you mean more to me than just a friend."

"Don't say 'just a friend.' Friends are very special and I'm lucky to have you as mine."

She was dropping clues the size of elephants, but he wasn't picking them up. He must have responded physically.

"Please don't get any closer, Carter."

"But we're meant to be together, Sally."

"No, we're not. Not in the way you mean. I asked you over here to request that you stop calling me. I appreciate your kindness, but I want to be alone with my grief for a while."

"But that's not right. It was only Gary that kept us from being together, and now he's gone."

"I miss him terribly."

"No, you don't. You just think you do. You'll realize that soon enough. He wasn't worthy of you. He was a mistake in your life. Forget him."

The longer he talked, the more forcefully.

"I can never forget him."

"I'll make you."

"You're hurting me, Carter. Let go!"

"But I love you."

"Let go!"

We all jumped up, three knights in rusting armor. Despite his bulk, Mac reached the pocket doors first and yanked them open.

"Stop!" he yelled, uncreatively. He held his Colt .32, but loose at his side and not aimed.

Carter Hastings, paramedic and taekwondo student, looked like Mac had hit him with a two-by-four.

"What the hell? What are you doing here?"

"Never mind that," Oscar said. "What you're doing in here is pretty clear—putting the make on the woman whose husband you killed."

That was a bit of an overstatement, maybe trying to compensate for Hastings's failure to make our life easy by confessing to Sally Lobring as Mac had hoped/expected.

"Killed Gary?" Hastings said. He looked at Sally, who appeared on the verge of collapse, then back at the trio facing him. Standing next to her, he was only slightly taller, with neatly combed blond hair and a buttoned-down shirt. He was dressed for a date. "Don't be ridiculous. I tried to save his life."

"He died by insulin, a most unusual murder weapon," Mac said. "Virtually anyone could have gotten access to the substance, to be sure. However, who would have *thought* of using it to kill? Most likely someone with medical knowledge, including the effects of insulin on non-diabetics. When Jefferson assumed that you were an EMT, Mr. Hastings, you corrected him and explained that vastly more training is required to be a paramedic. Another difference is that paramedics are permitted to administer drugs using needles and EMTs are not."

"So what? That doesn't prove anything. Chief, are you going to let him keep badgering me like that?"

"Hell's bells, yes. Go on, Mac."

Oscar knew what was coming. Most of it, anyway. Enough to pull him into the final act.

"Jefferson's account under hypnosis of the minutes surrounding the murder, as he witnessed them, is unimpeachable. All along he has been understandably haunted by the inexplicable fact that the murder apparently was committed in his presence while his eyes were on the victim for all but a few seconds, and yet he did not see it. As Sherlock Holmes said in 'The Adventure of the Priory School,' 'It is impossible as I stated it, and therefore I must in some respect have stated it wrong.' Once I began thinking of you as a suspect, Mr. Hastings, the truth suggested itself: You killed your beloved's husband with insulin inside the EMS vehicle, where it was readily at hand along with emergency medicines. There were others in the vehicle, but undoubtedly not giving you particular scrutiny."

"But he was dying when I got there!" Hastings protested. The words should have been convincing, but the manner wasn't.

"You implied as much at the time, quite surprisingly for a paramedic. Perhaps you uttered those ominous words 'I'm afraid he won't be okay at all' at the very moment you realized that the man you most wanted to see dead was in your hands—and the means to dispatch him not far away."

"You miserable bastard!" Sally spat at Hastings. "You pathetic low-life!"

He couldn't have looked any more shocked and hurt if she'd slapped him.

"However," Mac continued, "Gary Lobring was not dying when you arrived on the scene. He had simply fainted, as he had several times in the weeks before his death. Most likely he was anemic. That would be difficult to detect in an autopsy. Jefferson found his pulse racing, which Dr. Eppensteiner tells me would be the case with anemia. Of course, low blood sugar can also cause fainting. By the way, Jefferson, did Hastings attempt to revive the unconscious man? I thought not. An inconceivable lapse for a paramedic. Tell me, Hastings, did you ask whether Mr. Lobring was a diabetic because you thought that might have caused his fainting, as you stated? Or was it because you were already thinking of how to take advantage of the situation to remove the unconscious man who was such an obstacle to your happiness? It was of little consequence that Jefferson could not answer your question. You knew it was statistically unlikely that Mr. Lobring was afflicted with diabetes, meaning that insulin would therefore prove fatal to him."

Hastings turned sullen. "You've got no proof."

"That is a false assumption, Mr. Hastings. You should know quite well that Sussex County Emergency

Medical Services maintains a detailed inventory of all its vehicles' contents."

"I had a check made this afternoon," Oscar said, grabbing the metaphorical microphone. "The EMS truck that was in service at the parade on the Fourth of July is missing a vial of insulin. And there's no record that it was used on a patient."

"In a way, it was a magic trick, just as Jefferson intuited all along," Mac explained later that night, a couple of hours after Oscar took Hastings into custody and read him his rights. He was holding forth to Lynda, Kate, Sally, and me at The Speakeasy gastropub. Sally said she had to get out of the house for a while. Lynda couldn't have her customary Manhattan because of the twins (they were underage), but she destroyed a hot fudge sundae while we talked.

Mac turned to me. "You recall my reference to Penn & Teller's principle of simulation?"

"Something about believing is seeing, because the magician makes the audience think something happened which really *didn't* happen."

"Succinctly put, Jefferson! Yes, that is the essence of it. And that is what Carter Hastings did when he indicated that Gary Lobring was dying, when in fact he had simply fainted. I should have realized early on that was a possibility, given that you"—he nodded to Sally—"told us your husband had fainted several times recently. However, Hastings successfully created the illusion that the victim was already at death's door when he arrived on the scene. It is hardly to the discredit of the police that they never suspected the fatal blow was only struck later, inside the EMS vehicle."

"But Jeff"—Lynda affectionately put her left arm around me, the one that wasn't occupied with her bowl of fat and sugar with a cherry on top—"insisted all along that nobody could have injected Gary along the parade route without him seeing it. Shouldn't Carter have done the deed in a bigger crowd or something, where he wouldn't have been noticed and lots of people could have done it?"

"Indeed, he should have! You have a fine criminal mind, Lynda. However, Hastings had no choice. Remember, this was a crime of opportunity, conceived and executed within seconds. For that reason, I am confident that Hastings had not the slightest intention of creating the illusion of an impossible crime. Most likely he never even expected the murder to be detected."

"Then why pretend that Gary was already dying?" Kate asked.

"Possibly to make his death less surprising, and therefore less open to scrutiny. As an unintended consequence, however, the pretense also produced the impression that the victim was attacked before Hastings arrived on the scene."

"I still can't believe he did any of it." Sally appeared to be addressing her scotch. "He always seemed so nice."

"Covetousness is a powerful sin," Mac pontificated.

It made the top 10!

"He admitted to us that he had poor impulse control," I reported. "He said that's why he took up martial arts."

"Well," Kate said, "that didn't work very well, did it?"

Foul Ball

I

You could say that what the *Erin Observer & News-Ledger* alliteratively called "the Stadium Slaying" began with fireworks and ended with fireworks, just not the same kind.

When Oscar Hummel and I take in an Erin Eagles game, it's usually just the Chief and me enjoying the beer and baseball. But that night we had enough companions in the stands at Glad Tidings Stadium to stuff a clown car.

"I want a hot dog, darling," Lynda informed me. "And don't you dare tell me how many calories."

286—but that includes the bun.

"Yes, dear." I forked over the obscene price of a ballpark hot dog.

My wife looked quite fetching in her softball team's green and red cap, with her curly, honey-blond hair poking out the back in a ponytail. After bearing three children, she still has more curves than a mountain highway. Her teammate and best gal pal, Sister Mary Margaret Malone (Triple M to me and Sister Polly to the rest of the world), was decked out in a similar chapeau. Why their team was called the Gators, hundreds of miles from any such reptiles, is a mystery that might elude even Sebastian McCabe.

Mac was there, too, along with my sister Kate and my invaluable assistant Analiese "Popcorn" Pokorny, Oscar's significant other. But absent on that warm August 9 evening were the young Codys, ages two, two, and almost-four. They were in the tender care of their McCabe cousins because this was a date night for their parents. So why were Lynda and I not spending it alone in our whirlpool tub, after first throwing out the kids' toys? I wondered that myself.

Blame Kate for inviting us all for a group outing. She knows nothing about baseball and Mac, who was clad in a vast Erin Eagles T-shirt and a baseball cap that looked like half a deerstalker hat, knows slightly less. And yet they had two Eagles season tickets and a parking pass. That was their payback for hosting one of the players, pitcher Nestor Rodriguez, in the above-the-garage apartment I called home in my bachelor days. Kate had been roped into the unpaid B&B gig by her friend Moira Pargeter, volunteer host family coordinator. Moira had played substitute mom to Eagles players ever since the team moved to Erin three seasons earlier. The low pay scales of independent minor league teams like the Eagles made such zero-cost accommodations necessary for the players.

"Rodriguez couldn't pitch underhand," I heard Oscar tell Popcorn, his voice in lecture mode. "But Westwood is coming on strong as a slugger." He wore an Eagles cap on his bald noggin, as he does off and on, alternating with less conventional headgear when not wearing his official uniform hat.

"I'm only here for the fireworks," his inamorata (Mac's word) reminded him.

He whispered something in her ear. She giggled like a teenager, which she was about forty years ago. *You crazy kids.*

Fireworks on Fridays was new to the Erin Eagles experience this season, provided by Louisville, Kentucky-based Power Pyrotechnics from a barge on the Ohio River. The pinwheels, rockets, and whatnot were launched after the game and made an impressive display over the stadium.

"I love fireworks," Lynda said.

Before I could get in trouble by expressing a counter-opinion, the voice on the loudspeaker asked us to stand for the National Anthem. Rabbi David Goldman, one of three clerical tenors in the trio A Joyful Noise, belted it out with aplomb.

"Quite stirring," Mac pronounced it. But his words were drowned out by that truly thrilling call to arms—

"Play ball!"

Rodriquez gave up three runs to the Kitty Hawk Flyers in the top of the first, earning some choice "I-told-you-so" comments from Oscar. But catcher Chuck Westwood, Moira Pargeter's house guest, started a comeback in his first at-bat. After two balls and a foul, he hit a home run. The crowd went nuts.

"How's that for fireworks?" Triple M said.

First baseman Billy McAllister hit a triple, then was driven home on a sacrifice fly by outfielder De'Shante Smith. In the fifth inning, McAllister got tossed from the game for arguing, red-faced, with the home plate umpire about a third-strike call. The manager, Bob Oldendick, was also ejected.

"Good heavens!" Popcorn said.

"McAllister has a short fuse," Oscar told her unnecessarily. "He almost made body contact with the umpire. If he had, that would have meant a suspension."

"If only all violence could be dealt with so efficiently," Mac mused.

Westwood delivered two triples and another homer, this one with the bases loaded, contributing strongly to the final score of 9-5 over the Flyers. That brought the Eagles' game record to 48-34 for the season. They were in first place in the Western Division of the Liberty League, a twelve-team association which is not affiliated with Major League Baseball.

"I told you Westwood was coming on strong," Oscar said. "And none too soon—he's no spring chicken."

Nestor Rodriguez, on the other hand, only pitched the one inning and allowed three of the Flyers' five runs.

The post-game fireworks were beautiful, I must admit, and well-coordinated with the music. I just don't like the noise—the loud *bang! bang! bang!* But when Lynda put her arm around me and snuggled in response to the pyrotechnics, I didn't mind that part a bit.

Afterwards all seven of us adjourned to Bobbie McGee's Sports Bar in downtown Erin for beverages and conversation. Given the size of our party, and the night of the week, I was surprised that we didn't have to wait.

"Not too crowded tonight," I commented to Bobbie herself, who works all the high traffic times. Don't let the Stetson or the acres of wavy brown hair under it fool you. She didn't grab a degree from the Wharton School of Business by fluttering her long eyelashes.

"Friday nights when the Eagles are in town have been a little down this year," she explained. "That new rooftop bar at The Speakeasy has a great view of the fireworks. Thanks for stopping by."

Baseball was in Bobbie's blood by marriage. Her long-time husband, Brett McGee, is a Cincinnati Reds Hall-of-Famer. He owns a car dealership in the Queen City, but he prefers to live a quiet life in Erin.

We ordered our drinks—Caffeine-Free Diet Coke for me and hold the lemon slice.

"There's something really pure about minor league baseball," Triple M opined before her gin and tonic arrived. "Did you notice how the players were talking to the kids afterwards and signing their score cards? No big heads in this league."

"Our houseguest, young Mr. Rodriguez, certainly does not suffer from an outsized ego," said Mac.

"He ain't so young for a minor league ballplayer," Oscar pointed out, "and his performance on the mound is nothing to give him a big head about."

"Not to change the subject," Kate began, and went on to change the subject, as people will. About an hour and several topics later, I was about ready to call it a night. The four ladies of our party, on the other hand, were animatedly speculating on the private life of a reality-TV chef and his producer who were married. (Whether they were married to each other I have no clue, since I only listened long enough to know that I didn't want to listen.) Oscar looked relieved when his phone rang. That didn't stop him from growling his answer.

"Hummel! What? Hell's bells! I'll be right there." He was standing before he signed off.

"That was Gibbons," he announced. "There's been a murder at Glad Tidings Stadium. With any luck, I might beat the coroner to the body for a change."

Mac stood, too. "Come along, Jefferson."

II

When businessman Quincy Nicholson bought the Eagles and brought the team to Erin in 2016, the stadium was then called St. Hildegarde Health. But the hospital took its name off the sports palace two years later, citing an unfortunate number of ambulance runs there due to errant baseballs. Glad Tidings stepped into the breach. The non-denominational megachurch with a hip image bought the naming rights to the stadium for a reported $1 million. The city of Erin, meaning me and the rest of the taxpayers, own the facility itself. SBU's highly ranked men's baseball team also plays there.

We arrived in Oscar's cruiser to find the place as brightly lit as it had been during the game—with the added panache of two police cars and an EMT vehicle outside. Lt. Col. L. Jack Gibbons, Oscar's assistant chief, was talking to a tallish, barrel-chested guy with two chins, big glasses, and male pattern baldness. He was deeply tanned. What hair he had was graying and a bit long in back. Close up, I recognized the athlete-gone-to-pot as Eagles manager Bob Oldendick. They stood outside the perimeter created by the yellow crime scene tape. The body and the medical types, including the coroner, were several yards away.

"What's the deal, Gibbons?" Oscar asked.

"That's what I want to know!" Oldendick said.

My mental image upon hearing of the murder was an umpire beaten to death with a baseball bat, but Oscar debunked that on the way to the crime scene. The victim, a middle-aged male, was shot to death behind the stadium on the part of the property that was outside the admission gate, and therefore accessible to anyone with or without a ticket. A night security guard who found the body called the police and his boss, probably not in that order.

"The driver's license and credit cards indicate the dead man's name was Thomas Pargeter," Gibbons said, answering the Chief and ignoring Oldendick.

Mac raised an eyebrow.

"Pargeter!" Oldendick repeated. "That's Moira's husband."

"Soon to be former," Mac elaborated. "Mr. and Mrs. Pargeter were separated and in the midst of a very contentious divorce."

"How do you know all that?" Oscar demanded.

"Alas, this gossip was pressed upon me by Kate. You will recall that Mrs. Pargeter was the friend who convinced her to rent our apartment to Nestor Rodriguez."

"The lousy pitcher," I added for Oscar's benefit.

"I'm going to have to cut him loose," Oldendick confided.

"About damned time," Oscar informed him.

"Good evening, gentlemen. Or rather, good morning."

I turned around. Dr. Arlene Eppensteiner, wearing a white lab coat over pink shorts, must thrive on lack of sleep. She appeared cheerful, brisk, and ready to shake hands. Same old Arly—as she's known to the voters —only more so with her next election just a year and three months away. She's about my age, the north end of mid-forties, standing all of five-foot-one. Although I understand that most coroners delegate the role of death investigator, ours likes to go all hands-on in that capacity if she's available.

And speaking of hands, she grabbed each of ours in turn and addressed us familiarly until she got to Oldendick. She paused.

"He was just leaving," Oscar said.

"But—but," Oldendick sputtered. He finally came up with, "This is my home field!"

"This is a crime scene. I'm sure we'll talk to you more later, but for now, scram—unless Gibbons has some questions that can't wait."

He looked at his assistant. The laconic Gibbons shook his head.

Oldendick left, muttering.

"Time of death?" Oscar asked the coroner.

Eppenstiner brushed strands of dark, frizzy hair off her face.

"You know that's just a guestimate at this point, Chief. But, based on body temperature, post-mortem lividity, and the early stage of rigor mortis, I'm comfortable saying that the deceased died about two hours ago. And he was shot from a distance, based on the lack of powder burns on skin or clothing and the absence of gunshot residue."

Mac looked at his left wrist, maybe hoping for inspiration from that hokey Sherlock Holmes watch. "Two hours ago was a few minutes past ten. The fireworks would have been underway at that time, quite effectively masking the sound of the gunshots. That is most likely not a fortuitous synchronicity that just happened to work in the killer's favor. In addition, if the killer were in the stands, no one was likely to notice his or her departure during the fireworks display to shoot the gun."

"On the other hand," I said, "the killer might not have been at the game or have anything at all to do with the Erin Eagles."

Oscar glared at me.

"Just trying to be helpful, Chief."

"One other thing," Eppensteiner said. "The deceased had a bruise on his face, like he'd been in a fight sometime in the past several days."

III

"Helluva thing to happen," Nestor Rodriguez said. He helped himself to another hamburger, freshly grilled by Chef McCabe on the insanely expensive stainless-steel monstrosity of a grill sitting on his back patio. "And the suspect list is the immediate world, right?"

"Well, let us at least say the number of individuals with opportunity is not small."

Rodriguez said it better.

"For example," Mac continued, "you yourself probably could not prove where you were during the fireworks."

Rodriguez gave a boyish grin, even though he was well into his 20s. "Oh yeah, I could. I was in the locker room showering with my teammates. In the majors there would have been reporters around, too, but that never happens at our level."

"Were all your teammates present?"

"Yeah."

"Are you sure?"

"Where else would they be? I mean, after a game, you want a shower. Not that I can specifically remember each one being there. One shower after a game is pretty much the same as another. But some of them must remember *me*, if that's what you're getting at, because I was there."

Where else would you be? On an upper level of the stadium, shooting down?

This was late Saturday afternoon.

Before Mac and I left the Glad Tidings Stadium area the night before, we saw the body. Based on the blood, Pargeter looked like he'd been riddled with bullets. We found out later there were only three, all in the middle of his body, but that was enough. Oscar figured that a good shot could have plugged him from the stadium plaza while the crowd of almost 4,000 baseball and fireworks fans had their eyes glued on Power Pyrotechnics' handwork. Pargeter would have been a sitting duck in the bright arena lighting. And the noise would have been completely drowned out by the fireworks, as Mac observed early on.

In case you like timetables, here's one from Mac:

6:35—game starts
9:30—game ends
9:45—fireworks start
10:15—fireworks end
11:21—body found
11:33—Gibbons calls Oscar
12:05—Coroner examines body

"Motive won't be a problem, either," Kate said. "Tom didn't exactly have a personality designed to win friends and influence people. Isn't that why you asked to change host families this year, Nestor?"

Rodriguez nodded. My mother would probably think him a good-looking young man. He had dark hair and manners. He was less than medium height, but not as short as he looked out on the field.

"I cannot tell a lie," Rodriguez said. "Mrs. Pargeter is a sweetheart, but her husband was a jerk. They were still together at the beginning of the season and I didn't want to live with him again. He was always on my back last year, especially if I had a bad night."

"Ouch," Lynda said. She sipped her lemonade. I wore sunglasses as protection against her bright yellow tennis dress. Our kids were off playing with their cousins. "I can see where that would get your shorts in a bunch," she added.

My wife, the writer.

"I'm very concerned about Moira," Kate said abruptly. "I'm sure Oscar will suspect her of killing her soon-to-be-ex. I can read Oscar like a book."

"An illiterate could read Oscar like a book," I pointed out. "He's not subtle or inconsistent, God love him."

"We all love him," Lynda said. "That's beside the point. He does tend to go for the obvious in matters homicidal."

Such thinking had once caused him to consider me a suspect, but that was many years ago[11].

"Perhaps you could be of some comfort to her, Kate," Mac said.

"I was hoping that maybe you could get involved."

That's what she said in words. What she was saying to Mac with her green eyes, I didn't even want to think about.

Mac cleared his throat rather theatrically, a Wagnerian rumble. "Yes, well, I could speak with her, if you think that will help."

"Oh, thank you!" She gave him a hug, which required some stretching, and a kiss. "Of course, I knew you'd say that. That's why I invited her to come for dessert."

"I must have loved Tom once," Moira said over a calorie-laden bowl of Winter's double chocolate chip ice cream drowned in enough dark chocolate syrup to choke a horse. Comfort food. Lynda looked at it longingly. "After all, we have a beautiful daughter together. She's seventeen, almost eighteen. But that's hard to remember now, the love. Tom became so controlling—even jealous, though he had no reason to be. I call that mental cruelty. A few months ago, I

---

[11] See the first McCabe-Cody adventure, *No Police Like Holmes* (MX Publishing, 2011.)

finally had enough of it. I kicked him out of the house, which I inherited from my parents. Maybe we married too young."

She was an attractive woman, fortyish, with auburn hair—reddish brown, not real red like Kate's and mine—and fair skin with freckles. The lush hair was swept off her neck in a bun.

"What were your current relations, Mrs. Pargeter?" Mac asked.

"Moira, please. I'm trying to forget the Pargeter. His lawyer talked to my lawyer—that was our relations. Tom was trying to work out a settlement on the cheap. At the same time, he tried to get me in trouble at work by telling lies about me." Moira was a real estate agent for Happy Homes Realty. "And on top of all that, he tried to poison Freddie—that's our daughter—against me."

"How was that working out for him?" Lynda asked.

She smiled, showing a nice set of teeth. "It went over like a lead balloon. Tom and Freddie have never been close, and he made it oh-so-clear that he didn't like her boyfriend. My guess is that's the only reason she didn't ditch Roy months ago. Tom was deaf, dumb, and blind to think Freddie would take his side."

"I can see why somebody"—*Oscar Hummel, for instance*—"might think you'd want him dead," I said.

"Exactly," Kate put in.

"Nothing like that ever entered my mind," Moira fired back. "I just wanted him out of my life."

"Well, he is that," Mac said pointedly. "Did the police tell you that he was apparently shot during the fireworks?"

Moira shook her head. "No, but Kate did. I only spoke to the police briefly last night. I imagine they'll want to talk to me again."

"That scarcely requires imagination. They will undoubtedly ask where you were during the fireworks."

"I was watching from the press booth with a friend."
Alibi!

"The whole time?"

She nodded. "From beginning to end. But I'm not sure I should answer any questions from the police without the advice of a lawyer."

Kate cleared her throat. Maybe it was clogged with that sugary chocolate syrup, of which she had partaken as much as Moira. She'd put on a few pounds over the last few years. But I didn't say that! "The sooner Tom's murder is solved, Moira, the sooner you can get on with your life. Would you like Sebastian to look into it?"

"What? No. I mean, that hardly seems necessary. You don't need to go to the bother, Mac." *It's no bother.* "I'm sure the police will clear it up."

"Even so," Mac said, "I am by nature curious and cannot forebear to ask: Who do you think killed your husband?"

"Oh!" She set down her bowl. "This has all been such a shock I haven't really thought about that. Maybe it was an accident, a shot gone wild. Or maybe Tom had a business dispute with somebody. He owned what he called a 'tree health' business—Dr. Roots."

Somehow the idea of a dissatisfied customer plugging a tree surgeon didn't work for me.

"Pargeter and Oldendick didn't get along." This intervention from Rodriguez startled me. He'd been so quiet since Moira's arrival that I forgot he was there. "They traded barbs in front of me a couple of times when I stayed at the Pargeters' house last season."

Moira frowned. "That's true. Tom started it, of course. He didn't like my involvement with the team, from the manager on down. But I doubt if Bob Oldendick even saw Tom since our marriage broke up. Could I have a drink?"

"Of course," Kate said, standing as she spoke. "We have tea, soft drinks, beer—"

"Vodka, please. I need vodka."

IV

"It was very convenient of Rodriguez to point the finger at the manager who he probably knows is going to send him packing," Lynda observed that night in bed. "It's especially suspicious since he had his own run-ins with Pargeter."

"But why would he be so upfront about his bad blood with the dead man?" I objected.

"Somebody was going to bring it up sooner or later, so why not him? It was a great way to divert suspicion."

That was devious. She'd been around Mac and me too long.

"Maybe so, Lyn, but why kill Pargeter at the stadium, pointing right at the team, instead of on some neutral territory?"

"The murder site doesn't point to the team any more than it points to the thousands of fans there that night, even if Oscar's guess is right that the gun was shot from inside the stadium. Besides, Glad Tidings Stadium is an environment familiar to Rodriguez, so he could plan exactly how it was going to go down. The fireworks gave him perfect cover. All he had to do was lure Tom Pargeter there."

"So, you think Mac's house guest is the killer?" *The guy's staying in my old apartment. That's creepy!*

Lynda sighed. "Not necessarily. I'm just trying to do what Mac would do if he were on the case."

I lifted my head from the pillow to look into those gorgeous gold-flecked brown eyes, striving mightily to avoid the major distraction of what wasn't concealed by her sheer summer night-gown. "What makes you think he's not on the case?"

"The widow made it pretty clear she wasn't interested in Mac walking through the door that Kate opened for him."

I almost laughed. Not at the metaphor, possibly the result of Lynda's new day job as an aspiring novelist now that she was no longer slaving away for the Grier media empire. No, it was the notion of Sebastian McCabe needing to be begged into a murder that seemed risible. Admittedly, he usually postures about not wanting to interfere in police business and all that rot right up to the time somebody begs him to get involved. But I've always assumed that was just a fig leaf for doing what he wanted to do anyway.

The reference to Moira Pargeter made me think. "Kate had a good point when she said that a quick solution to her husband's murder would be the best way for Moira to move forward. Do you think it's suspicious that she didn't want Mac to investigate?"

"Not particularly." Lynda yawned. "Say, are we going to talk all night, or do you want to—"

"Let's not talk all night."

Mac called me late Monday morning. Popcorn and I were knee-deep in planning the communications aspects of Grant Kingsley's inauguration as St. Benignus University's seventh president in September. That would mark the end of his successful run as interim head honcho. There were a million details to manage in connection with the ceremony— news releases to write, speeches to draft, press credentials to print. This was a big deal in our world, something that hadn't happened in a generation.

There was plenty more on our plate as well, with the fall semester just two weeks away. It was crunch time.

"Are you free to join me in a visit to our beloved chief of police to exchange information about the Pargeter case?" Mac asked.

"Sure. I'm not busy."

Lynda would have rolled her eyes. Popcorn looked up from making notes on her laptop and smiled. "Happy sleuthing. I'll hold down the fort. Give Oscar my love."

"That's your job. How did you guess I was going to see him?"

"I didn't. I deduced it. The 'You're So Vain' ringtone told me it was Mac calling. I know Mac didn't call Oscar this weekend because I was with him—Oscar, that is—the whole time."

"Spare me the lurid details."

I was pretty sure there weren't any, but Popcorn stifled a giggle and continued. "Therefore, Mac called because he wants you to go with him to discuss the case with Oscar. Which means you are going to do that, leaving me to do the real work around here, as per usual."

Her reasoning had more holes than a loose-leaf notebook. She just got lucky, but I let that pass.

"Is there a problem with that?" I asked.

"Of course not, Boss."

Less than half an hour later, the big guy and I were outside Oscar's office trading pleasantries with Holly Burdette, his young assistant and guardian at the gate. She's a twenty-something gal with copper-colored hair in a pixie cut, a penchant for pearl earrings, and a boyish figure.

"What kind of mood is he in?" I asked.

"Let's put it this way: It's Monday morning and the Reds and the Eagles both lost yesterday."

Question answered. "You should put up a sign saying, 'Beware of Bear.'"

He didn't growl when we proceeded into his inner sanctum, though. My guess is his fifth cup of coffee made him suitable for company.

"You disappointed me," Oscar told Mac as an opening shot. "I had a bet with Popcorn that you'd stick your nose into the Pargeter shooting before the end of the day yesterday. I expected you to call while we were fishing."

Fishing! Popcorn really must love the old cuss.

"My apologies, Oscar," Mac said on the way to the Keurig machine to help himself. "I am already involved in the case by virtue of my presence at the crime scene on Friday night and our role as surrogate parents of sorts for one of the Eagle players. However, I saw no reason to disturb your weekend to discuss the matter—especially since you would be awaiting data from the coroner and the BCI.[12] What have you learned since last we met?"

"Funny you should ask. The BCI report just came in. Gibbons drove the bullet to the lab in London"—London, Ohio, that is—"early Saturday so we could get a quick read on it. Skipping the gobbled-gook and mumbo-jumbo, the gun was probably a 9mm. I'd guess a Taurus 709 or a Ruger SR9c semi-auto. Those weapons are narrow, compact, and easy to carry in a pocket. They cost less than three hundred bucks, but they almost always go bang when you need them to. These are very common weapons for middle-class folks."

"Not much chance of tracing the gun, I suppose?"

Oscar snorted. "What gun? It's probably at the bottom of the Ohio by now. That's a big river out there. But even if we found the pistol, there may be no record of the sale. Paperwork isn't required on sales between private individuals, including those at gun shows."

"And the coroner?" I said. "What did she have to say?"

"The autopsy confirmed Arly's original estimate on the time of death, so that whole fireworks thing holds up. Pargeter took three shots to the middle of his body, including one to his heart and one to his left lung. From the angle of the wounds, it's pretty clear somebody shot down from above. No telling how high above for sure, but my guess that

---

[12] The Ohio Bureau of Criminal Investigation (BCI) is the state's official crime lab, assisting local, state, and federal agencies 24/7.

it was from the stadium plaza works just fine. That's about all we have. There's not what you'd call crime scene evidence, given that the killer wasn't mano a mano with the victim."

I've put holes in cardboard targets with a borrowed .357 from time to time at the Bull's Eye shooting range with Mac, but I really know almost nothing about guns. "Would that be considered a long-distance shot that we're talking about?" I asked.

"The average shooter firing a pistol can hit a target fifty percent of the time at twenty-five yards," Mac put in. *Everybody knows that, Mac.*

"Okay. The stadium plaza is the equivalent of what— maybe five stories high? The distance from there to the ground would be more than twenty-five yards."

"Then he was a better-than-average shooter," Oscar said.

"He?" I repeated.

"Or she. Whoever. The killer."

"Perhaps," Mac allowed. "That is one explanation. What other avenues of inquiry have you pursued?"

I grabbed myself a cup of decaf and got comfortable in my usual chair.

"You must have seen Rawls' story this morning." Oscar pointed to the newspaper on his desk.

How could we avoid it? **POLICE SEEK HELP IN STADIUM SLAYING** was the headline atop the *Erin Observer & News-Ledger*, the murder getting banner treatment in our local paper of record for the second day in a row. (It happened too late to make the print edition on Saturday.) The story beneath Johanna Rawls' byline started with this:

Police Chief Oscar Hummel thinks that one or more of the 3,723 Erin Eagles fans attending Friday night's game at Glad Tidings Stadium may have information that could solve the murder of Thomas Pargeter.

"We're asking that anybody who saw anything that they now deem suspicious get in touch with us," Hummel said. "It may only take one conscientious citizen to solve this case."

Pargeter, 49, was shot to death . . .

"What do you think the chances are that will bring in anything?" I asked.

"Fifty-fifty."

Optimist.

"What else have you done?" Mac asked.

"We checked Pargeter's cell phone records, of course. Nothing helpful there. His calls were mostly to and from customers. He wasn't a desk guy calling the shots for some big operation. He went out and cut off tree limbs and so forth along with his three employees. So, customers called him directly and he called them, presumably confirming appointments. I have the names right here, all the calls for last week."

Oscar turned to his computer and clicked the mouse a few times before he read off the screen:

"Wendell Lyons, one call. Ben Stewart, three calls. Yvonne Jenkins, six calls. Sherman Cappel, two calls. Alicia Cook, one call. Cappel was an old buddy from high school. They were making plans to hoist a few beers together at Bobbie McGee's on Wednesday night, which they did. All the others said they were customers, either dealing with work in progress or setting up appointments.

"That was all just last week. Gibbons gave me the full monty, going back three months. You know how thorough he is. But it's just more of the same with different names. Pargeter hadn't called his wife in more than a month, though he did call his daughter a couple of times in that period. He also had a land line, though, so he could have called the manager of the Eagles and threatened his life for all we know."

"Have you interviewed Mrs. Pargeter?"

"Not yet. She lawyered up, which doesn't thrill me, so we'll have to work through her counsel. Evan Farleigh's daughter, Phoebe, apparently thinks Murder One is a good place to begin handling criminal defense cases. She was already the widow's lawyer in her divorce, at which she actually has some experience. Not much though. She just passed the bar earlier this year."

He knocked back his latest cup of coffee as if it were a shot of bourbon. "To tell you the truth, boys, I don't think much of Moira Pargeter as a suspect. She was already getting rid of the guy the legal way. I guess if she gets a bundle from his estate, I might rethink that. But right now, she's not at the top of my suspect list."

Mac raised an eyebrow. "Then who is?"

"Nobody yet. We're just scratching around. For instance, what if Mrs. Pargeter has a boyfriend with homicidal instincts who isn't happy with the way Pargeter is treating his almost-ex? That's one thing I'd like to talk to her about. Or the motive could be a business thing related to his Dr. Roots operation." *An unhappy tree!* "I'm having Burdette go over the victim's checkbook, business accounts, things like that as soon as I get a search warrant from Judge Kessler."

"Holly?" I couldn't help myself. "She's going to run the financial paper trail?"

"Don't sound so shocked. She graduated in business from Murray State University. Great head for figures."

"Then why is she your administrative assistant?"

"*Executive* assistant," he corrected me. "I promoted her. Besides, her dad is a cop in Paducah and she's working on her master's in criminal justice at SBU."

"A fine school, to be sure."

"Gentlemen, please!" For some reason, Mac had the air of a man most put-upon. "However, fascinating Ms. Burdette's academic career and lineage may be, can we get back to the point? What do you expect to find of significance in Mr. Pargeter's financial records, Oscar?"

"Who knows? Could be anything. Maybe he was taking regular payments from somebody, which could mean he was a blackmailer. Hey, that's not bad!"

"It has promise," Mac allowed. "Have you considered any member of the Eagles? After all, the murder took place at the team's back door, as it were. That can scarcely be a coincidence."

"Why not?" I countered. "If I wanted to murder somebody and get away with it, I wouldn't do it right behind my house."

"There is that, old boy."

"Anyway," Oscar said, "as far as we know at this point, Pargeter didn't have a connection to the team, except through his estranged wife."

"He did know Nestor Rodriguez and Bob Oldendick," I informed him. "Rodriguez made a point of telling us the manager and Pargeter didn't get along. On the other hand, Lynda thinks Nestor Rodriguez looks good for it. Or, at least, she test-drove that theory." I filled him in on our pillow talk, skipping the more piquant personal details. Mac had already heard it on the way over to the police station. At the end of my narrative, the Chief looked unconvinced.

"If you think there's any fish in those waters, have at it, you two. But I've cast my lines and I'm going to reel them in."

V

"What now?" I asked Mac once we'd settled into his vintage Chevy. "Oscar spouting fishing metaphors can't be a good sign."

"A trip to Glad Tidings Stadium seems in order, Jefferson. I grant your point that the scene of the crime almost counts against the likelihood of any team member being involved. However, we cannot discount the possibility that the killer is one of the players who expected law enforcement to come to that very conclusion."

My head started to throb. "Any plan in particular once we get there?"

"We have already met the manager, Mr. Oldendick, in somewhat strained circumstances. Now we should ask him a few questions. I do not say that I find Nestor Rodriguez's scenario convincing. However, it seems to me that a good manager would have his thumb on the pulse of the team. In other words, he may know something."

Mac pulled out his smartphone, Googled the team's name, punched in the number, fumed his way through the usual interminable recorded options, and eventually wound up talking to Oldendick. In the big leagues, I'm sure a manager wouldn't have answered his own phone, but the Erin Eagles are on a different planet from the majors. Erin's team is part of the Liberty League, one of the half-dozen or so leagues not affiliated with MLB and therefore able to locate close to major league franchises. But it's still pro ball, and alumni occasionally move on to the majors.

Mac neglected to hold the phone out to me or put it on speaker, so I only heard his side of the conversation.

"Mr. Oldendick? Sebastian McCabe here. We met the other evening. Yes, that was I with Chief Hummel. I was hoping you would remember me. Really? How very good of you to say so. Jefferson Cody, whom you also met, and I just came from Chief Hummel's office. We were wondering if you could talk to us for a few moments this afternoon. No, not about baseball. In conjunction with the murder. That may be so, I grant you. However, I can tell you from my experience that you may possess valuable information without being aware of it. Yes, I did realize that you have a game this evening. I promise you that our visit will be short. Thank, you, sir. We are on our way."

Mac hung up, a smile of success poking its way through the hair around his lips. He started the car.

"What do you know about Mr. Oldendick, old boy?" he asked over the roar of the V-8 engine.

"As it happens, a lot."

I'd gone to school on Bob Oldendick by calling Paul Baxter, the freelance writer who covered the Eagles for the *Observer*. I figured he might be able to tell me a few things about the manager that I wouldn't find online—i.e., gossip.

"Like a lot of minor league coaches and managers, Oldendick has a Big League background," I reported. "He played right field for six undistinguished years in the majors. In that period, he was on four different teams and was repeatedly sent down to the minors and called back up again. About twenty years ago he went to the minors for good, first as a coach and then as a manager. He worked for AAA teams, then AA, which are still part of the Major League Baseball system. He never played for, coached, or managed a championship team. Then he joined the Eagles."

"His career has not been a stellar one," Mac understated.

"More like a downward spiral. At this point, he's probably just glad to still be in baseball. Plus, the Eagles have a real shot this year at the division championship of their league. That's not exactly like winning a World Series, but it's something."

I pulled out my phone and answered five or six emails. Hadley Reams, the *Observer*'s new education reporter, wanted to know if it were true that the School of Arts and Humanities was being renamed in honor of our new president's predecessor, the much-loved "Father Joe" Pirelli. I answered in the affirmative with some satisfaction at the young reporter's initiative. Not so long ago, Hadley was the editor of our campus newspaper, *The Spectator*. He seemed to be launched on a successful career in journalism, no mean feat these days.

Bob Oldendick's office on the second floor of the stadium was decorated with bobbleheads, signed baseballs, old photos, and a few trophies. He was the biggest thing in it, with his chest straining the buttons of his uniform shirt. That wasn't muscle.

He came from behind his desk to greet us, pumping our hands as he cut to the heart of the matter.

"Tell me again what your role in this mess is, McCabe!"

He seemed to mostly talk in explanation points, and louder than necessary. Also, he never asked us to sit down and make ourselves comfortable.

"Completely unofficial," Mac assured him.

"And yet you're connected to the Erin police!"

"As you noted, we were with Chief Hummel on the night of the murder." Mac doesn't lie when he can avoid it, but I thought he was being overly ambiguous and even evasive there. In a certain sense, we *are* connected to the police. The Chief has even called us special deputies on occasion. Plus, my assistant is practically joined at the hip to the man. But if Oldendick assumed that our association with Oscar meant that the law sent us to see him, that was his mistake.

"I still don't get what you want with me!"

"We would like your perspective on certain relationships. For example, Nestor Rodriguez apparently did not get along well with the dead man."

"Who did?"

Fair point. Not his wife, clearly.

Mac ignored the rhetorical question. "By Mr. Rodriguez's own account, the deceased was prone to heckling comments about him when the former was the latter's house guest."

Got that?

Oldendick looked jarred. "You're not seriously reading anything into that, are you? Sportsmen at every level of every sport get that kind of crap all the time! And mostly from people who haven't got what it takes themselves— damned armchair athletes! And don't even get me started on sports writers!"

"How about Billy McAllister?"

"Is this a change of subject?"

"Not quite. I observed that your first baseman seems to have what these days is popularly called an 'anger management issue.'"

"No shit, Sherlock!" Oldendick stared at the ceiling. I doubt he was praying. "So Billy gets a little hot under the collar! So what! He's a kid, fresh out of OU. He'll grow up."

Don't count on it. Not all athletes do.

"Wrath can quickly turn to shouts and even shoves on a baseball diamond," Mac pontificated, as if he spent his off-hours squeezed into a stadium seat or glued to ESPN. "When firearms are involved, however, the result can be deadly. Did Billy McAllister have a particular animus toward the deceased?"

"I doubt if he even knew him."

"Did you?"

"Know Pargeter? Sure, I knew him!"

"I meant, did you have a particular animus toward him?"

Oldendick snorted. "Other way around! The horse's ass accused me of hitting the sheets with Moira!"

Mac raised an eyebrow. "You mean he suspected the two of you had an amorous relationship?"

"That's what I said!"

Moira had neglected to mention this.

"And I presume from your tone and word choice that this suspicion was groundless?" Mac put it as a question.

"Damn right! Nothing to it at all! We're just good friends."

How often had I heard that? Sometimes it was even true.

"I noticed you called Mrs. Oldendick by her first name," I said, just to keep my hand in.

The manager looked disgusted, and somehow older. "Don't be nuts! How many women do *you* call by their first names? Moira and I are friends, period. She sold me a house when I moved here from Pennsylvania three years ago. My contract with the Quaker City Starlings and my third marriage expired at about the same time, so I caught a break when this job opened up. Anyway, long story short, I talked her into being one of our host families for the players because I could see she had the right personality. She took to it right away. She's been a real mom-away-from-home for those guys! Never misses a home game unless she has to show a house that night!"

"And that was the extent of your relationship with Mrs. Oldendick?" Mac pressed.

"That's it!" A crooked smile appeared above his chins. "Mind you, I'm not saying I would refuse any generosity in that direction. Moira has more than just a nice personality going for her." He didn't waggle his eyebrows, but I got his point. "She didn't send any signals in my direction, though, so I figured she was stuck on her husband. Shows you what I know! They broke up and she got a boyfriend."

If Mac had had a cigar in his mouth, it would have fallen out. "She told you this?"

"She didn't need to! It's obvious! I've seen her acting more than a little friendly with Baxter ever since she and Pargeter split! Paul Baxter, that is—that guy who covers us for the *Observer*. Did I tell you I hate sports reporters? But, hey, don't read too much into the boyfriend thing! I'm sure Moira didn't, you know, have anything to do with killing her husband!"

"No, of course not," Mac agreed heartily.

VI

"The boyfriend wasn't a good thing for Moira to forget to mention," I said as we made our way to the stadium elevator. "It looks bad."

"That is undeniable." Mac looked glum, his usual ebullience on hiatus.

Afternoon was heading toward evening. Oldendick had invited us out of his office because he had a game to manage. We decided to stay and watch, hoping for a vibe that would stir up a storm in the McCabe brain.

"Moira did tell us that she was in the press box with a friend during the fireworks," Mac mused. "It is scarcely to our credit that we did not pursue the friend's identity."

"So, she and her 'friend'"—air quotes—"alibi each other. That doesn't help Moira much. Not that I can see Paul Baxter plugging somebody. He's a nice guy. But we've known nice killers before."

Helen Calloway's, for instance. The solution to Dr. Calloway's murder was a wound that I never expected to heal.[13] While I was remembering that awful business from the previous December with sadness, the elevator doors opened on the familiar form of Rabbi David Goldman. He's an ursine figure, about sixty years old, with light brown, curly hair. We all shared content-free greetings of the sort common to casual friends.

"What brings you here?" I asked after the ritual, although I knew that the rabbi (a) played baseball in college,

---

[13] See *Too Many Clues* (MX Publishing, 2019).

(b) remains a rabid fan, and (c) sang the national anthem in this very stadium on the night of the murder.

"I just stopped by to see if I could be of any spiritual help to the players," Goldman explained. "Murder within one's orbit is a traumatic episode, even if one is not directly involved."

Tell us about it, Rabbi.

"Without breaking any confidences," Mac said carefully, "can you say whether any of the players seemed particularly affected?"

He shrugged. "Who can really tell? The dead man was not one of their own, so it is perhaps not surprising that only one player was visibly moved. We talked a bit about the shortness and uncertainty of life. The Book of Wisdom has quite a bit to say about that."

"Indeed. 'Vanity of vanities.' And who was that one player, Rabbi?"

"Billy McAllister. I believe he is the youngest and least experienced player on the team. He certainly is the most emotional."

Amen to that! Although "hot-headed" also works.

"While you were counseling him, you could have thrown in anger management," I joshed.

Rabbi Goldman smiled. "That is not within my competence."

Mac and I moved on to the game. McAllister behaved himself this time, while racking up a single, a double, and a triple. There should be a special statistic for that. Westwood kept up his streak with a double, two triples, and his fourth home run in three games, a rocket out to center field. Nestor Rodriguez, on the other hand, rode the bench.

Most importantly for Mac, this was Mystery Night at Glad Tidings Stadium, a special promotion to boost attendance. The gimmick was that at the end of every inning, actors in costumes popped up somewhere in the stadium and traded dialogue with each other. A mystery in eight acts, you might call it. The fans in the stands were given little pads of paper to write down clues and submit a solution, dropping their deductions in special containers around the stadium. Winning entries were eligible for a shot at free tickets to the Liberty League's Western Division Championship Series. Entries containing the correct solution went into the hopper for a raffle, with five lucky winners to be chosen.

"I can't believe they didn't cancel this nonsense," I told Mac, "given the real murder on their doorstep."

"It does seem rather insensitive, I grant you."

"Maybe some marketing genius figured that Mystery Night, coming on the heels of the Pargeter shooting, would pack 'em in."

If so, that person figured right. The 4,200-seat stadium did seem fuller than on the previous Friday.

The Mystery Night storyline was hokey, not that I haven't read worse. Heck, I've *written* worse. Here's the scenario: The setting is 1930s Chicago. Private eye Dick Hardstone is hired by a pint-sized night club owner called Wee Willie to spy on his girlfriend, the headliner at his club, and find out if she's cheating on him. Just as Hardstone reports back that Willie's fears are justified, Willie gets shot by a mysterious androgynous figure.

Inning after inning, popping up in different sections of the stadium, the intrepid PI interviews various characters. They all supply clues: the feckless girlfriend, the girlfriend's other suitor, Willie's wife, Willie's thieving business partner, the recently promoted homicide detective on the case, the mob boss, and the Salvation Army girl who hangs out near the night club looking for lost souls.

"Surely this is a variation of 'the detective did it,'" Mac posited. "By that I mean the homicide detective. No doubt he accepted bribes from Wee Willie before his ascent in the force and now he wishes to cover that up so he can rise even higher."

"As you might put it, that strains credibility," I protested. "What cop in that time and place *wasn't* on the take? No, I bet the Salvation Army girl did it."

"For what possible reason, old boy?"

"Didn't you get her reference to her fatherless son? Every child has a father, and I bet this one looks a lot like Wee Willie. He done her wrong."

"Plausible, I must admit. Well, if you are right, Jefferson, I will buy you the beverage of your choice."

And he did! For the first time ever, my solution to a crime was right and Mac's was wrong. After the eighth inning my suspect tearfully confessed that, in a moment of weakness, she plugged the man who seduced her in a moment of weakness. I didn't win tickets to the Liberty League playoffs, but baseball beer never tasted so good!

"This has not been a productive day, Jefferson," Mac complained as he watched me down my celebratory brew. "And yet somehow I have the feeling we have been handed a significant clue if only we had the wits to see it!"

The next day, Tuesday, was an off day for the Eagles, and we managed to catch Moira at home around noon. I mentally logged the foray as my lunch hour.

She lived in a three-bedroom brick two-story in a thirty-year-old subdivision barely within the Erin city limits. Not only was Chuck Westwood in the house when we arrived, but also Moira's daughter Freddie (for Winnifred) and Freddie's boyfriend, Roy Drinkwater. Apparently, they'd been having a chat fest in the family room, just off the small entranceway.

"I apologize for our intrusion," Mac told Moira after she let us in with a look of surprise on her face. "Despite your notable lack of enthusiasm for the endeavor, I have been making inquiries into your husband's death."

From her downturned mouth, I deduced this was not welcome news. "And what did you find out?"

"Hey, maybe I should go," Chuck Westwood said, looking about as a sheepish as possible for a handsome blond-haired guy whose muscles had muscles.

Roy Drinkwater glanced up from his phone. "Good idea." He was tall, skinny, shaggy-haired, and up to that point totally immersed in his phone. Freddie shot daggers at him with her eyes. She looked a lot like her mother, minus a couple of decades and a load of worries, with the same shade of auburn hair. Freddie was just a few weeks away from starting her senior year at Malcolm C. Cotton High, according to Kate.

Drinkwater went back to looking down at the device in his hands.

"Please stay, Chuck," Moira said, ignoring the byplay between the daughter and the boyfriend. "Go on, Mac. What did you find out?"

"For one thing, I learned that you have formed a new romantic attachment which you neglected to mention to me."

"Paul?" I gave her points for not pretending puzzlement. "Why should I tell you about him? What does he have to do with anything?"

Had the woman never watched *Law & Order*?

"He's just a nice man who works at the blood bank and covers sports for the paper," Freddie put it.

"I am sure he is a fine fellow," Mac said. "Jefferson assures me as much. However, I fear the suspicious nature of the police will be aroused when they find out you have an amorous relationship with a man who is not your husband."

"But it's not amorous." She stopped. "Well, to be honest, I guess it is. It's just not serious. Or, hell, maybe it is now."

"Good for you, Mom!" Freddie said, not sarcastic but enthusiastic.

"But it didn't start out that way! We were just friends until I kicked Tom out. Then things changed. And why not? Just because my marriage was dead, that didn't mean I had to be." The line had the ring of something she'd said before, maybe to convince herself. "Paul makes me laugh. I haven't laughed a lot in the last ten or fifteen years. I don't know why I'm telling you this."

"Did your husband know about your new attachment?"

"Yeah. And that bugs the hell out of me because I can't figure it out. Paul and I have been very discreet pending the divorce. Our public dates, if you want to call them that, have all been in the press box at Eagles games. How would Tom know that? He never went to games, even before we split. But he threw my friendship with Paul in my face when I ran into him at Lawrence's IGA a week or two ago, like it was some scandalous romance. He told me I would pay for it in our divorce settlement."

"That sounds like Daddy," Freddie said.

"I never met the guy," Westwood said, "but he must have been a real piece of work."

"You have no idea," Moira said. "But I wasn't worried about his threats. When I told my lawyer what he said to me, she laughed."

Mac fingered his beard. "Well, that is a moot point now that Mr. Pargeter's death has obviated the need for a divorce. Do you know the terms of his will?"

Moira gave that a thought, glanced around, then rendered her verdict: "I've said too much already. I'm sure you're trying to help, Mac, but I just realized that when Phoebe told me not to talk about the murder without her being present, that applied to you, too. And I'm paying too much for her legal advice to ignore it. How's Kate?"

VII

"So, the great amateur came up empty-handed, eh?" Oscar seemed by no means displeased by this observation next morning. He sat back in his chair and contemplated Sebastian McCabe across the desk, his hands on his ample corporation.

"Not exactly," I said, springing to Mac's defense. "There is the whole boyfriend thing. And maybe there's a reason Moira clammed up just when Mac asked about her husband's will."

"Perhaps it has escaped your notice, Jefferson, that Kate did not ask me to implicate her friend in this matter," Mac said heavily. "In fact, I am quite certain that such an outcome would result in unhappiness for Kate and consequent unpleasantness for me in my domestic relations."

Having known my sister all my life, I can believe that.

"Married life must be hell," said Oscar, who most likely will never know. Not while his mother is alive, at least. "Is that all you got since I saw you last?"

"We also talked with Bob Oldendick," Mac said. "He reported that the deceased accused him of having an illicit extra-marital relationship with Moira Pargeter, which he asserted was untrue. It was he who brought up the name of Paul Baxter as Mrs. Pargeter's true love interest. However, his account is consistent with her insistence that their friendship only developed into something more after the breakup of the Pargeter marriage."

"Humph. More importantly, does Oldendick think the Eagles will take the Western Division championship?"

"That, I neglected to ask."

"Westwood has been burning up the ball lately—more homers this month than last season total."

"Next time we see him, we'll congratulate him," I said, hoping Oscar recognized the sarcasm. But I'm pretty sure he didn't. "Westwood's power hitting might be relevant if Pargeter was beamed with a baseball bat, or if he knew the dead man—which, so far as we know, he didn't."

The Chief just looked at me.

"I concede that Jefferson and I have not covered ourselves with glory in this case," Mac said. "Perhaps you have done better."

Oscar smiled as if he had just won a bet on a nag at Sussex Downs paying 20-1. "Maybe I have."

"A big response from your appeal in the *Observer* for conscientious citizens to come forward?" I asked. I doubted that because "the Stadium Slaying" had moved off the front page of the *Observer* and on to the local pages and the letters to the editor. Tall Rawls' story *du jour* on the subject was a profile of the victim, Thomas Pargeter, who was described as a quiet neighbor and a good tree surgeon. Mrs. Moira Pargeter, who might have contributed a different viewpoint, declined comment for the story. The editorial page sported a couple of letters from citizens who posited that if Glad Tidings Stadium wasn't safe from gunfire, no place was safe. Similar sentiments populated the twittersphere.

So, my question was half-rhetorical and half-jibe. If Oscar had picked up an eyewitness because of his appeal in the *Observer*, the paper wouldn't have kept that secret. Unless the Chief was holding out on Erin's premier crime reporter.

But he wasn't. "Response, yes. Help, no. Just the usual load of crap on the half-shell—a junior high kid suspects his science teacher, an elderly lady called to say we need stronger gun control laws, a man says his former partner is both a gun nut and a tree-hugger who might have a grievance against 'Dr. Roots,' etc., etc., etc. Gibbons actually took a run at the tree-hugger, but he was at an Orange Zebra concert in Cincinnati with his new love interest on the murder night."

"Lynda loves that band."

"I'll make a note of that. Oh, and the mayor visited. It seems the villagers are getting restless, seeing as how Pargeter could have been the victim of a random shooting by a nut. Reverend Mayor Sutterlee respectfully urged me to step on the gas with this investigation. As if we're idling."

And yet, Oscar didn't look down in the dumps.

"Other lines of inquiry were more successful, I take it," Mac said.

"You take it right. For starters, Holly Burdette found out that Pargeter spent a wad of money at Electronics-R-Us right when he was in the process of moving out under orders from his wife. I mean several K, not what you'd drop on buying a new computer or something like that. In fact, his computer was a two-hundred-dollar H-P laptop."

"How do you know all that?" I wondered.

"Burdette and Gibbons searched the dead man's apartment, as per the warrant signed by Judge Kessler. Apparently, Pargeter was no great housekeeper, considering that they found his credit card bills for the last two months in his underwear drawer. He also had a gun, a Ruger LCP, stuffed inside a sock. It wasn't the murder weapon."

"What do you think his electronics purchases portend?" Mac asked.

"I don't have the slightest idea." Oscar gave his hands a workout for emphasis. "But it might mean something. Why would a guy just moving into a bachelor apartment— meaning he's going to need dishwashing crap and stuff like that—fork over all that dough on tech? It's an oddity."

"Indeed," Mac said, "and oddities are never to be ignored."

"Yeah, well, here's an even odder oddity," Oscar said. He was enjoying himself. After a dramatic pause, he said, "Billy McAllister is a phony."

Okay, I'll bite.

"What do you mean, a phony?" I asked before Mac could.

"His official biography on the Eagles' website doesn't check out. No Billy or William McAllister played ball for Ohio University in the relevant time period. In fact, nobody of that name attended the university in the last five years."

Mac raised an eyebrow.

"That's impossible!" I objected. "I mean, the team would know all about his track record in college ball." The Cody memory banks kicked in. "The manager even referred to him being 'fresh out of OU.' What does Oldendick say about this? What does McAllister say?"

"They're on a road trip to Bay City, Michigan. I think the Eagles can take the series. They're back on Saturday. I'll talk to them then. I want to do this in person."

VIII

"What's your best guess about what's up with McAllister?" I pressed Mac when we were out of Oscar's earshot.

"Like Sherlock Holmes, I never guess."

"Of course you do. You just call it theorizing or speculating."

"Speculation, which is hardly the same as guessing, would be futile at this point in the absence of data."

"Maybe he really did play for OU, only under a different name," I speculated. "Suppose Billy McAllister is the son of Pargeter's sworn enemy and changed his name to hide his identity when he wormed his way onto the team so he could knock off Pargeter in revenge."

Mac looked at me with disdain. "Are you trying to goad me with that ineffable twaddle, Jefferson?"

"Or maybe he's Pargeter's secret son," I theorized, undaunted. "Remember, I was right about Wee Willie and that Salvation Army girl."

Where did this highly creative theorizing come from? Blame Lynda's passion for watching *Midsomer Murders*. Season after season, that show is full of motives involving hidden parentage, revenge, or both. Personally, I could never swallow the idea that there would be so many homicides in small towns.

"There may be a much simpler explanation which eludes even your inventive brain," Mac said. *I think that's sarcasm.* "We shall see on Saturday what Messers McAllister and Oldendick have to say."

"And what about Pargeter having a gun? Do you think he expected trouble?"

"*Au contraire*, Jefferson. If he feared for his life, he would hardly keep his firearm concealed in a sock. He would keep it on his person, with or without a concealed carry permit."

I couldn't argue with Mac's logic. "But don't forget the coroner said Pargeter had a bruise on his face. I don't think that came from a love tap."

"Undoubtedly not. And yet, to posit that the same person is the author of both assaults on the victim seems a bridge too far without further data." Mac changed the subject. "I have the distinct feeling, which I have had during some of our other investigations, that I have heard something important and I do not know what. Not today, but at some point. Oh, well. It is firmly lodged in my subconscious mind for now. Eventually it will emerge from hiding. Meanwhile, I believe a conversation with Paul Baxter is in order."

"Why?"

"Because he is the third side of a romantic triangle, old boy, and one of the other two sides has been shot to death."

We found our man at his day job, the blood bank on High Street. Freelance writers do all kinds of other things for steady income. Paul Baxter has been a high school sports reporter for the *Observer* since he was in high school himself. He added the local pro baseball beat when the Eagles landed in Erin (from Chagrin Falls, where the team was formerly known as the Beavers before Quincy Nicholson bought it). I knew Baxter through Lynda, who was his boss when she worked at the paper as news editor.

He was one of three employees hard at work on donors when we entered the facility, sticking them with needles and such. I tried not to look. Baxter is shorter than Moira, with a receding hairline, a pencil mustache, and a slight build. He wore a white lab coat (which evoked the coroner in a not-especially-pleasant memory) and a ready smile. We had to go through a front-line employee to get to him— receptionist or some such.

"Have you ever given blood before, Mr. Cody?" she asked in that bored manner of a person rattling off the same words so often they've almost lost their meaning.

"No, I haven't, and I—" *have no intention of doing it now.*

"My friend is a bit nervous about the process," Mac interrupted.

"A lot of people are the first time," the receptionist said. She was so skinny she looked like she could use some blood herself.

"Give us a moment," Mac told her.

We walked away a few feet. "You will notice that Mr. Baxter and his associates are surprisingly busy today," Mac said. That was true. Even though there were there two such associates, about four times that number of generous folks sat around waiting to make a deposit in the blood bank. "I very much fear that the only way to speak to him right now is to become a donor. I assure you the process is easy and virtually painless after the initial prick."

"If it's such a cake walk, then why don't you do it yourself?"

"Alas, I donated blood five weeks ago. It is too soon to do so again. Surely you are not frightened, old boy?"

"Frightened? As in scared? Of a little needle and a little blood? Don't be silly." I chuckled, as if amused at the very thought. *Uneasy, maybe. I'll admit to uneasy.*

We returned to the receptionist.

"Are you sure you want to do this?" the receptionist asked me.

"Certainly, he does," Mac told her in a cheerful tone before I could speak for myself. "Mr. Baxter is a friend of his."

She granted me a professional smile. Her lipstick was a little off, but the color was right—a vivid shade of red. "I'll make sure Paul draws your blood."

We had to wait about half an hour, during which I checked email, the Dow Jones Industrial Average, and the always-depressing national news. I also fielded a text from Popcorn:

How goes the sleuthing, boss?
Like giving blood.

Mac was right. The needle didn't hurt much, once Baxter finally found a vein by beating all over my arm. I wondered whether I was going to have bruises.

"Isn't your wife a friend of Moira's?" he asked Mac as he began to connect the plastic bags that would hold the life's blood flowing out of my arm. "I'm still shocked about Tom getting murdered."

Funny you should mention that little incident, Paul.

Mac opened his mouth to ask Baxter a question, but he didn't get a chance. Baxter rolled on, continuing to make this surreptitious interview virtually effortless on our part.

"Not to speak ill of the dead"—*always a sure sign that the speaker is about to do so*—"and especially a man I never even met, but I hear from Moira that her husband was a real skank. He was trying to blame me for the breakup so he wouldn't have to pay a big divorce settlement. And I had nothing to do with it, believe me."

"Define big," I said. Numbers always attract my attention, especially when they are preceded by dollar signs.

He shrugged. "Search me. All I know is, it wasn't like that and I didn't appreciate being dragged into it. I'm a widower. Lost my wife two years ago next month. Sweetest woman who ever lived, Shari was. She and Moira were friends. Since she died, Moira's been checking in on me a few times a week. Just being a good friend to her friend's widower. Well, after she broke up with her husband, that changed things a little. I guess you could say we're dating, if they still call it that. I sure never saw that coming! It just sort of happened."

I could see why Baxter wrote sports instead of romance novels.

"Clearly you care for Mrs. Pargeter very much," Mac said.

"Yes, sir," he said softly. "That I do. She's a wonderful woman. And she loves baseball." I wasn't sure whether that last quality was the icing on the cake or the cake itself.

Baxter disconnected a plastic bag full of my blood and wrote on it. It's a good thing I don't faint at the sight of the red stuff, especially mine.

"Your affection for her being what it is," Mac said, "you must be pleased that this thorn in her side has been extracted permanently."

It took him a second to process that. "Tom Pargeter, you mean? Well, yeah, I'm sure glad he's not bothering Moira anymore, though I guess this means she gets no alimony." *You could say that. But there may be an inheritance.* "Plenty of other people feel the same way, you know. About him being out of the picture, I mean. Not about Moira."

The woman in the chair on my right, on the hefty side and in need of a tune-up on the blond in her hair, looked our way. The expression on her face said she wished Baxter would speak louder.

"People such as?" Mac probed.

"I remember Moira telling me last season that Nestor Rodriguez groused to her about Tom. That's why he's not bunking at the Pargeter house this year. And there's Freddie's boyfriend—Freddie's the daughter, you know. The boyfriend, his name's Roy Somebody, and Tom couldn't stand each other. From what Moira said, that's Roy's major attraction for Freddie. She and her dad were oil and water. When the family was together, Moira's main job was referee. At least, that's how it seems from what I've heard."

Charming.

"What about Chuck Westwood?"

"He's on fire! If he can keep it up, he could wind up in the majors someday. That's not common for a player from the independent minor leagues, but it's happened before—Jose Canseco, Rickey Henderson, Daryl Strawberry."

Mac didn't look enthralled at this intelligence. "I appreciate your expert opinion on Mr. Westwood's career prospects. However, I was wondering whether he also was among those negatively disposed toward Mr. Pargeter."

"Didn't like him, you mean? Oh, I don't know about that. Did he even know him? Tom was already out of the house when Westwood came to stay there. He sure is favorably disposed toward Freddie, though."

"Is he indeed?"

"Yep. And the boyfriend doesn't like it one bit."

"I kind of picked that up," I said, remembering Roy Drinkwater's attempted put-down of Westwood during our visit to the Pargeter house.

"How about Billy McAllister?"

"I don't think he knew Tom, either. He's new to the team, and Moira and Tom broke up right before the season started. In fact, I don't even know if he knows Moira. She's never mentioned him to me that I can recall. Billy's another player with potential, by the way. He's got a temper, but that's never ruined a baseball career yet."

"What do you know about his background before he joined the team?" Mac asked.

Baxter shook his head. "Not much. Played for Ohio U, if I remember correctly."

By this time, I'd given more blood than one of Dracula's victims. I was feeling a little light-headed. Maybe that's why Paul Baxter, clearly head-over-heels for the newly minted widow, seemed to me at that moment as likely a killer as anybody else we'd questioned.

"Do you own a gun?" I asked him. Sometimes a sudden question like that, out of the blue with no tilling the ground in advance, produces an off-the-cuff honest answer.

"A gun? Good heavens, no! I hate the things. I won't even go to the range with Moira."

Mac raised an eyebrow. "The range?"

"She belongs to a gun club," Baxter explained. "All women."

IX

The offices of Farleigh & Farleigh have been located on Main Street since long before I came to Erin. That's where we met with Moira and her lawyer, Phoebe Farleigh, who became the "& Farleigh" just a few months previously. Phoebe's father, Evan, originally held that position behind *his* father and kept it open for her until she passed the bar exam that February.

"I'm sorry to put this on such a formal basis, Mac," Moira said. "I know you're just trying to help."

"Don't apologize," Farleigh told her briskly. Then, to Mac: "Given your close relationship with Chief Hummel, the only reason we're talking to you is that my client is happy to cooperate with the authorities in every way possible. I consider this discussion semi-official. If the Erin police wish to have a more formal interview, I will schedule one as soon as it's convenient for my client. I have already spoken briefly with Assistant Chief Gibbons to answer a few questions that he had. I assure you, Professor McCabe, that my client wants her husband's murder solved as quickly as possible so that she can move on with her life."

If you've formed a mental image of Phoebe Farleigh as a surly cigar-smoking gargoyle based on this monologue, scratch that and shame on you. Farleigh was in her late twenties, with a full head of soft brown hair and eyes to match. She wore a cream-colored blouse and a chocolate-colored skirt. Her make-up was flawless, and her cozy office tastefully decorated, right down to the faux leather visitor chairs into which Mac and I sank. There was something appealing to me about her businesslike approach. It beat phony sweetness to hell and back, in my book.

"Moving on would include carrying out the dispositions of the deceased's will, I presume," Mac said mildly.

She didn't bite. "So far as we can determine, Ms. Pargeter's husband died intestate. One of Gibbons' questions was whether my client was in possession of a will. He asked this because no such document was found among the papers in the deceased's apartment."

"We never got around to making one," Moira stuck in. "I don't think Tom liked to think about dying. He didn't have life insurance, either."

Her counsel glared at her. "The fact that you didn't know about a will may be indicative, but it's not definitive." Back to Mac: "The deceased was represented by the Bridges Law Firm in his business matters. So, I checked with Jim Bridges to see if he executed a will without my client's knowledge. He did not. Presuming that Mr. Pargeter didn't use another attorney to write such a will, then Ohio law dictates that half of his estate will go to his widow and half to his daughter." She almost smiled. "I think that's eminently fair, don't you, Professor?"

Mac nodded. "Eminently. However, has it occurred to you that suspicious minds might think that proviso gave Mrs. Pargeter an excellent motive for hastening her husband's demise before he *could* execute a last will and testament—one that disinherited her?"

"That's a cute theory, Professor, but in practical terms you can't really disinherit a spouse in the state of Ohio." Farleigh shifted into lecture mode. "The state recognizes that disinheriting a spouse could cause great hardship, particularly if there are children involved and the surviving spouse isn't the greater wage earner. So, Ohio inheritance law provides for something called 'elective share.' In simple terms, a surviving spouse is always entitled to at least what he or she would receive if the spouse died intestate. In other words, my client could only have benefited if her husband made a will, not suffered from it. Who knows? Perhaps he would have been racked by guilt and left her a substantial sum."

Oh, come on!

"Not very likely, I grant you," she added, maybe in response to the look on my face.

"In any case," Mac said, "Mrs. Pargeter profits by her husband's death."

"By that logic every married man should go around with an armed guard."

Moira, who had sat through this interchange looking like a POW, recaptured the ability to speak.

"I thought Kate said you would help me, not accuse me of murder," she threw at Mac.

He raised an eyebrow. "My dear Moira, I accuse you of nothing! Surely you understand that I am merely stating the obvious. For the moment, Chief Hummel is exploring avenues that do not involve you. However, if they turn out to be dead ends, I feel confident that he will turn his attention your way. He may become very interested in your hobby, for example."

"What hobby?"

"Shooting guns."

Farleigh laughed, and it wasn't forced. She was genuinely amused.

"I never thought of it as a hobby, exactly," Moira said. "I belong to WASP."

She said that as if it meant something. It didn't to me. "What's that?" I asked.

"Women Armed and Set for Peril," Mac supplied. "I suspect the acronym came first, and the rather tortured name built around it."

"Very good, Professor," Farleigh said. "If you know about our little group—yes, I'm a member as well—then I'm sure you know there are associations of female gun owners all over the country. We meet twice a month for instruction, practice, and sisterhood. Our members range in age from fifteen to seventy-eight. The oldest, Amy Hunt, carries a gun in her fanny pack when she goes for walks. There's nothing new about women choosing to take control over their own safety. I secured a concealed carry license four years ago after I was robbed at knifepoint while walking to my car at eight o'clock at night."

You must be a fun date, Phoebe.

Lynda would never do that; she's allergic to guns. Besides, she could taekwondo any footpads who tried to set upon her.

"Tom got me started," Moira said. "He owned a little Ruger and he taught me how to shoot." *That must have been the gun that Oscar's troops found in one of Pargeter's socks!*

"I am a firearms owner myself," Mac said. "May I ask what weapon you prefer, Moira?"

"Beretta 92 semi-automatic," Farleigh answered for her. *Didn't James Bond carry a Beretta until M took it away?* "It could have been the murder weapon, from what I read in the *Observer*. But it wasn't."

My phone pinged with an incoming text. It was from Lynda: *how's it going?*

"My client is quite willing to turn over her gun to the police for ballistics analysis upon request," the attorney added.

Slow, I informed my wife.

then hurry home—it's nap time

She didn't just mean for the kids. Suddenly I found it hard to concentrate on the interview. I sent her an appropriate response, never mind what.

"Moira could own more than one gun," Mac was saying. Or something like that. My mind was elsewhere.

"We could talk hypotheticals all day long, Professor," Farleigh retorted, sounding bored. Maybe that was a tactic.

"Do you have any questions for my client that might actually help solve the murder?"

"Perhaps. Do you know anything about Billy McAllister?"

"The Eagles first baseman? Just that he's pretty good and he has a temper. I've only met him casually."

"Did your husband know him?"

"Not that I'm aware. Why are you asking about McAllister?"

"He has attracted our attention for two reasons I would rather not specify at this point." *Namely, his temper and his false identity.* "Have you given any further thought to who might have wanted to kill your husband?"

She looked at Farleigh, who nodded slightly to indicate that she could answer.

"Other than me on a bad day?" *Probably not the answer Farleigh was expecting.* Moira shook her head. "No."

"Perhaps there was a current or former Eagle player who regarded you as a surrogate mother, and who realized that you would benefit both psychologically and materially by your husband's demise."

This was a new theory, and one that Moira Pargeter didn't buy. "One of my boys killing Tom on my account? I just can't wrap my head around that."

Mac switched approaches. "Mr. Pargeter spent a significant quantity of money on electronics shortly before he died. Do you have any idea why?"

"Electronics?" Her face and tone of voice both indicated surprise. She thought about it. "Tom wasn't into computers, sound systems, or anything like that." She thought about it some more. "Maybe he was spying on me. He knew about Paul somehow, even though we haven't paraded around town a lot. And he told Freddie he knew everything I was up to."

X

"That sounds far-fetched to me," I told Mac later. "Maybe Moira's paranoid."

"Can you think of any other reason why the deceased would invest a significant amount of money in electronic devices, given his modest residence and lack of interest in high-technology endeavors?"

"We only have his wife's word for the latter," I pointed out, "but, no."

"Nor can I. Where that fits into the puzzle, however, I have no idea."

And there it sat with no further action by Mac while we waited for Oldendick and McAllister to get back to Erin with the team.

The next two days, Thursday and Friday, I burrowed into work at SBU and put my Watson hat on the shelf. I drafted a Rotary Club speech for our president emeritus Father Joe, wrote a press release for the upcoming season at SBU's Davenport-Lattimore Bijou Theatre, and provided Hadley Reams with some statistics about the incoming students for the new academic year. My own work done, by early Friday afternoon I was looking over Popcorn's shoulder.

"Don't you have a mystery to solve?" she said finally. What a kidder.

Knowing when I wasn't wanted, I wandered over to Mac's office in Herbert Hall. He was at his desk typing an essay, or a syllabus, or a novel, or something.

He looked up. "To what do I owe the honor of your presence, old boy?"

"You're stuck on the Pargeter murder. Obviously, you need me to solve this thing, just like I did that Mystery Night caper."

"That would be most welcome, I assure you."

I took a seat and assumed a thoughtful pose. "If only Pargeter had a partner, or a girlfriend, or a Salvation Army—"

"Girlfriend!" Mac all but shouted. "By thunder, that must be it, Jefferson!"

"Eh? Must be what?"

"What my subconscious mind knew that I did not know. I trust you remember the phone calls on Thomas Pargeter's smartphone in the week or so before his murder, as related by Oscar?"

"I remember that they were all business, except for one high school buddy."

"So the other parties to those calls said. However, Pargeter was in contact with one woman six times in that short period, far more than any other customer."

"And you suspect monkey business rather than tree business?"

Instead of deigning to acknowledge this wordplay, Mac called Oscar and shared his suspicions.

Late that afternoon, Oscar's office was a full house. In addition to Mac and me, his guests were Yvonne Jenkins and her husband, Jerry Jenkins.

Mrs. Jenkins was pretty, but she didn't know it. She wore no make-up, although her brunette hair was nicely coiffed, and she was neatly dressed in a red blouse and black slacks. She was in her late thirties and had just begun her fifteenth year of teaching fourth grade at Our Lady of Knock School.

"I didn't exactly lie to Colonel Gibbons when he interviewed me," she said. "I just didn't tell him everything. I was too embarrassed, and the full story wouldn't exactly boost my career in Catholic education."

"You had a dalliance with Thomas Pargeter?" Mac asked.

She blushed and looked at her husband. He was a handsome, athletic-looking guy with a nice head of prematurely graying hair. He squeezed her hand.

"Not as I would use the word 'dalliance,'" she said. "It was more like a bit of a flirtation. The whole sorry business began when we needed a diseased tree taken down. Mr. Pargeter came and looked it over. Jerry wasn't home at the time. He—Mr. Pargeter—came back a second time, also during the day. He said some very flattering things to me. He was out of line and I should have told him, but it was nice hearing it. Then he started calling me. I let that go on much longer than I should have, even though the calls were short and I never called him. My mistake. I admit that. One day I handed Jerry my phone to look up a number and he noticed all the calls from Mr. Pargeter. He asked me what was going on and I told him the truth."

"Maybe if I'd paid more attention to my wife—" Jerry Jenkins began.

"Let's not go down that road again," she told him.

Jenkins operated the local Edward Jones office, which apparently involved sometimes working longer hours than the trading day on Wall Street.

"So that's all there was to it?" Oscar sounded skeptical.

"That's all," Yvonne Jenkins said. "I swear it."

"Well, there was one more thing," her husband said. "Just a few days before he was killed, I paid Dr. Roots a visit and told him to lay off."

"How did he take it?" I asked.

"Not too good. He, uh, questioned my ability to satisfy my wife. I punched him in the face."

"Well, that explains the bruise on the corpse," Oscar said. "Where were you a week ago today, the night of the murder?"

"Yvonne and I were together at the Forty Thieves Casino in Cincinnati." The smile on Jenkins' face suggested a fond memory. "We checked in for the weekend to, uh, get reacquainted."

"You enjoy gambling?" Mac asked.

"Not especially, but we didn't get around to leaving the room. If you check with the casino, they should be able to confirm we had room service for dinner and breakfast. Champagne, too."

Yvonne Jenkins blushed again.

XI

After they left, Oscar shook his head. "Pargeter was coming on to a customer at the same time he was accusing his wife of hanky-panky in hopes of not having to cough up a big divorce settlement. What an ass."

"Hardly a paragon of virtue, to be sure," Mac said.

But we already knew that, so all we'd accomplished by interviewing Mrs. Jenkins was to embarrass her. Not being one to belabor the obvious, I kept that thought to myself.

On Saturday, the Eagles were back from their road trip to Bay City and I was at Mac's house early in the A.M. In view of Oscar's stated plan to interview the pseudonymous Billy McAllister upon the team's return, Mac tapped the Chief's number on his smartphone to find out where that stood. He held out the phone so I could hear their conversation.

"Yeah, I called McAllister on his cell yesterday to tell him I wanted to talk to him this morning," Oscar reported. "Rosalie Hawthorne gave me his number—he's staying with her family. He blew up at first, but then he backed off and agreed to talk on one condition: He wanted Oldendick to be in the room. That suited me fine because I'm interested in hearing that gentleman's excuse for circulating what he had to know was a lie about McAllister's background. So, in half an hour I'm going to see what a baseball manager's office looks like." Oscar paused, then added casually, "You can come along if you want."

The *if* was a nice touch, I thought.

Billy McAllister sat slumped in a chair, gloomily clinging to a can of Red Bull. I don't know why he didn't just inject caffeine intravenously.

"This is all very easy to explain!" Oldendick said. But he was sweating, as people carrying a good deal more than a few extra pounds often do.

"I'm glad to hear that," Oscar said. "So, explain."

"My real name is Billy McGee," the first baseman announced. He seemed to think that meant something.

"And?" Oscar prodded.

"Brett McGee is my uncle."

Brett McGee! In Erin he's Bobbie's husband, but to the rest of the world he's the Cincinnati Reds Hall-of-Famer. The resemblance between nephew and uncle was slight, but there if you looked for it—the dark hair, the handsome face. But he didn't have Brett's smile, invariably described as "boyish" by cliché-prone sports writers.

"Growing up in Pittsburgh and playing ball at OU it didn't matter so much," McAllister went on. I'll call him that to keep it simple. "But now that I'm playing in Uncle Brett's back yard, I didn't want the family connection hanging over me. For every Ken Griffey Jr. who makes it bigger than his old man, there's a Pete Rose Jr. He spent most of his career in the minors and he got into trouble—"

"That has nothing to do with you!" Oldendick interrupted. I should hope not! In the early 2000s young Rose was sentenced to a brief term in prison after being convicted of distributing performance-enhancing drugs to his teammates in the late 1990s. PEDs were a big scandal in pro baseball around that time, a period sometimes called the "steroid era." Some people say that era never ended.

"Billy leveled with me from the beginning," the manager told Oscar. "I promised him I'd keep his secret as long as I could. The rest of his biography is all true!"

From the deflated look on his face, Oscar bought the whole benign explanation.

"That all seems innocuous enough," Mac observed. *Translation: Not a secret somebody would kill for. Except maybe a macho guy with "anger management issues."* "Do you own a gun, Mr. McGee?"

"McAllister, please." He chugged Red Bull. "Are you kidding? With my temper? I wouldn't trust myself with a gun."

"We're working on that!" Oldendick said. "Not a gun—Billy's temper!"

"Did you know the late Thomas Pargeter?" Oscar asked McAllister.

He shook his head vigorously. "I didn't even know he existed until he didn't."

Oscar turned his attention to Oldendick. "What do you think about the team's chances—"

The door banged open.

"What the *hell* are you doing harassing my manager and my first baseman?" the new arrival demanded.

I'd never met Quincy Nicholson, owner of the Erin Eagles, but his photo appeared prominently in the team's program along with a letter in which he welcomed the fans and mentioned that he attended every home game. Nicholson made his pile in the construction business, which is not for sissies. He was tall, corpulent, with a broad, black face accented by a white mustache and a white goatee. On this morning of August 15, he wore a three-piece bespoke suit, slate gray with pinstripes, that must have set him back four figures.

"We're trying to solve a murder, that's what," Oscar informed him. "And your employees are very wisely giving me their full co-operation."

"You didn't check with me first," Nicholson told Oldendick—unnecessarily, I'm sure. "I just found out from your secretary."

Oldendick looked more uneasy than I would have expected from a winning manager. "Sorry, I didn't think." *That's never a good thing to say, Bob.*

Nicholson eschewed the obvious comeback ("That's obvious") and turned back to Oscar. "And besides, they had nothing to do with the murder."

"How do you know?"

"Stands to reason, doesn't it? The victim wasn't a player, coach, sports reporter, bat boy, or fan. He just happened to be shot outside my stadium." *That's the Erin taxpayers' stadium, Quincy.* "So, obviously, my boys weren't involved."

"That remains to be seen," Oscar volleyed back.

"And in fact, there was a connection to the team through the victim's wife," Mac corrected Nicholson. "She has hosted players for several years and recruited others to do so. She is also a friend of Mr. Oldendick. Perhaps you already knew all that."

Instead of responding to the implied question, Nicholson let loose with: "And just who are you?"

Oldendick hastened to introduce us. Maybe he was trying to assert himself. He hadn't been talking in exclamation points since his boss barged in.

"Oh! I've heard of you," Nicholson told Mac. Surprisingly, he pumped his hand. "Pleasure to meet you, McCabe. What did I interrupt?"

"We were just discussing Mr. McAllister's true identity."

"Oh, *that*." Did Nicholson really think it was no big deal or did he want us to think it was no big deal? I rated that a tossup. "It's going to come out eventually—a big reveal, lot of publicity. It'll be a good thing, right?" He patted McAllister on the back.

The fallen jaw on McAllister's face clearly indicated this plan was news to him. He took a swig of his Red Bull and threw the can across the room into a wastebasket, looking sullen.

"I appreciate your dismay at the Eagles being pulled into a murder investigation," Mac told the team owner. "It is not as if you yourself had any connection with the dead man. Or did you?"

Nicholson give his mouth a rest for a few moments while he thought that over. Then he said, "Wasn't he a tree man? I think that's what I read in the paper."

"A tree surgeon, yes."

"I may have hired him once to work at my house." *A disgruntled customer!* "I'd have to check to be sure it was him. Either way, I sure as hell didn't *know* him. Look, I like publicity. I *love* publicity. But not this kind, the team mixed up in a murder. People are saying the stadium area isn't safe. I called the mayor about it. You need to solve this case, Chief—or you, McCabe—so people will stop that kind of talk. It's not only bad for the team, it's bad for the city."

Before Oscar could archly reply that solving the case is just what he was trying to do with this interview, my PR genes instantly kicked in. It's true that there were a relatively large number of Facebook postings and tweets implying that the stadium area had become something akin to the O.K. Corral, only more dangerous. But that didn't mean the posters represented anybody but themselves. The publicity could have cut largely the other way.

"How are ticket sales?" I asked Nicholson. There had been three home games in the week and a day since the murder, and another two coming up that night and the next.

"Well, they're up," he conceded. "But they should be up even more. We're in first place in the Liberty League and we're going to take the Western Division championship at least, with a good shot at the whole thing. Plus, Monday night was Mystery Night. That always pumps up attendance."

I solved the mystery, Quincy.

"You're sure about that championship?" Oscar asked.

"Damned sure, Chief. Right, Bob?" He looked at Oldendick, who—to give him credit—didn't cringe or look away.

"Damned right, Mr. Nicholson!"

"I don't like to lose," Nicholson said. "Not in business, not in sports."

This was not exactly Surprise of the Week.

"In view of your very understandable desire that the Erin Eagles not be associated with the Pargeter murder, I am rather surprised that you allowed the Mystery Night to continue," Mac said. "Surely that event called attention to the recent real-life mystery just outside the stadium."

I'd call the expression on Nicholson's face rueful. "Big mistake on my part, despite what I said about it as a fan draw. My community relations manager advised me to shit-can it for this year. Good advice. I should have taken it. But the contract with the actors didn't have an escape clause, so I would have had to pay them. The only thing I hate worse than losing is wasting money. The blowback from the fans wasn't worth it, though. Insensitive, folks said. Long-term, that's not a good image."

Play Santa Claus at Christmas and people will forget.

After that the meeting kind of limped to a halt, like a car with a flat. Nobody had any more questions. Oscar reassured Nicholson that the interview with his manager and first baseman was routine, provoked by McAllister's phony name. Nicholson said he understood, and he gave us all free tickets to prove it.

"More paperwork," Oscar muttered as we left the stadium. "I have to file a financial disclosure report with the city saying I accepted these tickets worth—what?—ten bucks when you buy in advance?"

"Fourteen," I said. "Those are VIP tickets, right behind home plate."

"Oh. That's worth it then."

Oscar's phone burst out into a *Mission: Impossible* theme song ring tone. I wish I'd thought of that one.

"Hummel! He does, does he? Well, tell him I'll get there when I get there. I'm on the way, but don't tell him that. Thanks."

He disconnected.

"That was Holly Burdette. There's a young man camped outside my office and refusing to leave until I see him. Wants to talk about the Pargeter case. He says he's Freddie Pargeter's boyfriend."

XII

"Your executive assistant works on Saturdays?" I asked Oscar as we left the stadium.

"Just today. I authorized a half-day of overtime for her to catch up on some regular duties she couldn't get to while she was pouring over Pargeter's finances."

"You hate administration, don't you?"

"It's not what you'd call my long suit."

He ignited an e-cigarette. That used to be considered safer than the real thing, but not so much in the summer of 2019 as vaping deaths piled up. I made a mental note to mention that to Oscar when I judged him to be in a receptive mood. I'm still waiting.

We found Roy Drinkwater sitting in one of the uncomfortable chairs in the Chief's outer office, his nose deep in his smartphone. My guess is it wasn't making him any smarter.

"Good morning, Chief, Mac, Jeff," Holly Burdette said in her usual cheerful manner. She was Saturday-dressed in jeans, which somehow made her look even younger than her early twenties.

We good-morninged her back, although there wasn't much morning left.

Drinkwater stood awkwardly, which was his style. His sandy hair overflowed the collar of his Cotton Cougars polo shirt, spirit wear from his and Freddie's high school.

"You wanted to see me," Oscar told him in his most authoritative voice.

"Chuck Westwood killed Freddie's dad." The words flowed out in a torrent, as if Drinkwater were afraid that if they didn't get out right away, they never would. "I'm sure of it."

"That's a very serious charge, young man," Oscar lectured. "Come into my office."

We all did so. Oscar took a mug and went to work on the Keurig machine. Drinkwater declined the offer of coffee, Mac picked up his **I SEE NO REASON TO ACT MY AGE** mug that Oscar kept on hand for him, and I contemplated fixing myself a decaf cappuccino.

The Chief settled himself into his padded chair with Drinkwater in front of him. "Now, what makes you *think* Chuck Westwood—who's on one hell of a hitting streak, by the way—killed your girlfriend's father?"

"Freddie's dad was waiting for us outside school one day. He told her not to let Westwood get into her pants. He said Westwood probably had a girl in every town where he played."

Mac raised an eyebrow. "How did he reach the conclusion that Mr. Westwood had made approaches to his daughter? The deceased separated from his wife before the baseball season started and, as I understand it, has had little contact with his family since. Presumably he was not in a situation where he would see Miss Pargeter interact with the gentleman in question."

The kid shrugged his scrawny shoulders. "I don't know how he knew, but he even quoted something Westwood said to Freddie. 'You're a very pretty girl,' or something lame like that. Freddie's been kind of distant with me ever since Westwood moved in. She denies having a thing for him, but I'm not so sure."

That would explain Drinkwater's coldness to Westwood the time I'd seen them together at the Pargeter house. It also gave the boy a good reason to try to implicate Westwood in the murder.

"And that's all you've got?" Oscar asked.

"Um, yes."

"And it couldn't wait until Monday? What's so urgent?"

Again, the shrug! "I don't know. I've just been thinking about it a lot and I had to get it off my chest."

"How did you get along with Pargeter?" I asked.

His eyes widened at the question and he looked from me to Oscar to Mac. "Not too well. He wasn't a fan of mine. Why?"

"Did you kill him?"

"Of course not."

"Well, you had about as much reason to kill him as Westwood did."

"That is to say, not much," Mac observed. "It seems to me that Mr. Pargeter had more reason to kill Mr. Westwood than vice versa."

"Maybe he tried to, and Westwood shot him in self-defense."

"That won't wash," Oscar said. "He was shot from a distance." But I could tell that he was struggling with himself, as if arguing internally whether he should say what was on his mind. He finally voted yes.

"On the other hand," he added, "let's not be so sure Westwood didn't have a motive. Suppose he got beyond first base with Freddie, maybe at some point after her father warned her off him. And Pargeter found out about it and confronted Westwood. Freddie's only seventeen, a minor. Unlawful sexual conduct with a minor is a felony in the fourth degree in Ohio, unless the perp is less than four years older than the minor. That could mean doing serious jail time. Somebody might kill to avoid that."

XIII

"Maybe you shouldn't have speculated about Chuck Westwood and Freddie in front of the kid," I told Oscar after Drinkwater left.

"Probably not."

Mac had ducked through the doorway with his phone out. He was gone probably ten minutes. Oscar and I talked about baseball, Popcorn, fishing, *Spider-Man: Far From Home*, and why everything that tastes good is bad for you. Maybe it was more than ten minutes.

"What's up?" I asked Mac when he returned.

"I telephoned a friend and asked him to meet us at the Pargeter home. Then I belatedly called Mrs. Pargeter to ask if she would admit us, explaining my reason. She called Phoebe Farleigh, who gave her permission with the proviso that she be present."

Got all that?

"What exactly did you explain?" Oscar asked before I could.

He explained.

A short while later, Freddie opened the door for us. Farleigh was already there, casually but tastefully garbed in a light summer dress. No flies on her! We quickly moved into the nearby family room.

"Maybe you'd better go watch TV or something," her mother told Freddie. The girl pouted. Westwood wasn't blowing smoke if he called her pretty.

"Or perhaps not," Mac said. He addressed Freddie. "You might be interested to know that your boyfriend visited Chief Hummel earlier this morning."

"What for?"

"To accuse Chuck Westwood of murdering your father," Oscar said.

She closed her eyes. "I am so mortified." She opened them again. They were a lovely shade of green, pairing nicely with her auburn hair. "How did he reach that brilliant conclusion, Chief?"

This is where it was going to get sticky.

"He said your father was convinced that Chuck Westwood made, uh, amorous advances at you." *You've been around Mac too long, Oscar.*

"Oh, that's ridiculous," Moira snapped.

Farleigh, surprisingly, didn't say anything. She looked interested, as if she wanted to see where this was going.

"Is it?" Oscar asked Freddie, not Moira. After all, she's the one who would know.

"Weeeell." Freddie dragged the word out.

"Answer the question and tell the truth," Farleigh said. "You have nothing to fear. If Westwood did anything to you –"

"He didn't! I mean, I suppose you could say he flirted a little by saying nice things to me." *That word "flirted" again.* "But that's all! He never touched me or asked me to do anything. Actually, I think he's a little shy around women."

"That's the impression I had," Moira contributed.

"Roy's just upset because he's not getting any," Freddie added. *TMI!* "And he's not going to. In fact, I'm just looking for a kind way to tell him we're through." *None of my ex-girlfriends ever worried about being kind.* "That would have made Dad happy."

And with that, she started bawling. Was she suddenly grieving for her father, or for the relationship she never had with him?

Her mother hugged and patted her.

When that wound down, Mac cleared his throat in the way that people do when they're about to say something. Then he spoke to the room at large:

"Roy Drinkwater's account of what the deceased told his daughter strengthened my conviction that he had exact knowledge, more than just second-hand information, about what was said in this house for some time after he –"

The doorbell rang.

Moira opened the front door on a man who must have been well into his seventies, with thinning grayish hair and multiple bellies. He had an electronic gizmo in his hand. Google the terms "hidden camera finder" or "hidden microphone detector" and be surprised at how many varieties there are. Before the newcomer could open his mouth, Mac said, "Ah, Richard! Thank you for coming."

"Pleasure, Mac."

He handed out a business card to each of us:

MOBARRY INVESTIGATIONS
Specialists in Electronic Surveillance

Contact information filled the reverse side.

"This is a wild goose chase," Moira averred. "As looney as Tom was, I can't believe he bugged the house."

"It may sound fantastic, but he must have had some way of keeping an eye on you and Freddie," Farleigh said. "Or an ear."

"Do you want to show me around?" Mobarry looked eager. I knew his background from Mac. He'd been a caterer in the Cincinnati area until he took classes at a whacky private eye school in the early 1990s.[14] After that, he turned his electronic eavesdropping hobby into a new career based in equal parts on keeping up with technology and staying (just barely) on the right side of privacy laws.

"Starting with your bedroom is a good idea," he added.

"Do not, however, forget the guest room," Mac said.

"I was never in Chuck's room with him," Freddie said hastily.

"Never?"

"Weeeell, I may have stood in the doorway once or twice while I was talking to him."

"At which time he called you pretty?"

"Maybe."

"Follow me," Moira directed Mobarry. "Just you." They left. The ever-vigilant Phoebe Farleigh, knowing the brush-off didn't include her, went with them. The rest of us stayed in the family room and out of the way.

"I don't get how this could have anything to do with Dad's murder," Freddie said. "I told you, Chuck didn't touch me. What are you after?"

Good question!

"Your father may have heard something else in the course of electronic eavesdropping, with fatal consequences for him," Mac said.

"Heard something like what?" Oscar asked.

"I have the beginnings of a notion about that, but it requires further consideration."

Instead of lapsing into a meditative pose, which I half-expected, Mac asked Freddie about her college plans. She said she wanted to go to a big school in a bigger city and study engineering. Mac offered a few suggestions while I tried to imagine what else Pargeter might have learned from

---

[14] See *School for Sleuths*, Wildside Press, 2018.

bugging his former home. If you have any ideas, you're ahead of me.

We moved on from that subject to several others in succession. We were discussing Oscar's poor taste in clothes when Mobarry, Moira, and Farleigh returned.

"This house has more bugs than a crack house," Mobarry announced. It sounded like a well-used line. "There are hidden cameras and microphones in the master bedroom and in the guest room. That computer in the kitchen? It was set up with software to copy all of Mrs. Pargeter's emails and IMs so her husband could read them. The girl's room is clean, but I bet this one isn't."

"I am so pissed," Moira fumed.

Mobarry went over the family room with his gizmo and quickly announced there was a camera right above a painting of a seascape. Who even looks at paintings once they've been hanging a few years?

"Spying in a wireless world is easier than it's ever been," Mobarry said.

"But isn't it illegal?" Moira asked her attorney.

That's kind of a moot point now, what with Pargeter being dead and all.

Farleigh shook her head. "Not necessarily. For example, both Ohio and federal law permit audio recording as long as one of the parties in the conversation knows about it. Your husband probably installed all this while he still lived here, and thus he would have been one of the parties in many cases. Another problem is that most laws are silent on video because it just wasn't an issue until recently. There have been some rulings against babysitters who sued over being monitored by 'nanny cams' in the child's home. Courts say they don't have the right of privacy they would in their own home."

"But this is *my* home," Moira protested.

"It was also your husband's, like the counselor said," Mobarry pointed out. "I got caught up in a case just like this in Cincinnati, must have been ten years ago. Knowing that he was heading for a divorce, the guy bugged his wife hoping to find out something he could use to strong-arm her into a favorable divorce settlement. You could say she took it poorly when she found out. She sued. The case dragged through the federal courts for so long I lost sight of it."

"My belief is that Thomas Pargeter installed electronic surveillance in this house for exactly that reason or something very like it," Mac said. "No doubt he was hoping to find salacious evidence of a romantic relationship involving his wife."

"That bastard!" the wife in question asserted. "If he wasn't already dead –"

"Go on," Farleigh instructed Mac, shutting off her client in mid-sentence.

"The deceased did, in fact, learn that his wife was being courted. He no doubt hoped that would be to his financial disadvantage in the divorce. Since he died while still married, however, Moira will share his estate with their daughter. Her alibi for the time of his death is a man to whom she has become enamored."

"That's a crock!"

"No, Ms. Farleigh, those are facts—facts which might appear damning if presented to a jury. However, it is also a fact that there was a camera and microphone in the room where Chuck Westwood is staying, leading to the likelihood that the deceased overheard conversations between Mr. Westwood and Freddie."

"But that was innocuous, I told you," Freddie said.

Mac nodded. "And, I for one, do not question your veracity on that point. However, I believe that your father overheard another conversation—or perhaps more than one—involving Mr. Westwood. I was hoping that the latter would be here this afternoon."

"He left right after you called me," Moira said.

Mac's eyebrows shot up. "Did he know that we were on our way? And why?"

"Yes, as a matter of act. I told him. I thought it was such an unbelievable idea that I laughed about it."

Mac didn't look amused. "Did he say where he was going?"

"Yeah. To Bob Oldendick's house."

"Hell and damnation! Why did I not ask you that earlier? Oscar, Jefferson, we must go there at once. I can only hope that we are not already too late!"

XIV

Moira gave us Oldendick's address—the house she sold him as a real estate agent.

"I'll have Gibbons meet us there," Oscar said, whipping out his phone.

Less than a minute later, we were on the road in Oscar's cruiser with the siren blaring and a light flashing on top.

"So, what the hell do you think Pargeter overheard?" he asked Mac.

"I strongly suspect it was a reference to performance-enhancing drugs, which led him to an ill-fated attempt at blackmailing the wrong person."

"Juicing!" I exclaimed. "How do you figure that?"

"How many times in the past week has Oscar referred to Chuck Westwood's recently increased—one might even say 'enhanced'—prowess at the bat? That strong performance this month has helped position the Eagles to win their league's division championship, and perhaps the ultimate prize as well. And do you recall what happened, Jefferson, when you attempted to reference Peter Edward Rose Jr.'s trouble with the law over a matter of distributing performance-enhancing drugs?"

I thought back. "Oldendick cut me off before I could finish the sentence. You mean he's protecting Westwood? Then why the hurry to get to his house?"

We were there before Mac could answer. Oldendick lived only a few minutes from the Pargeter place, in a modest brick ranch house on a cul-de-sac. Oscar, who can move surprisingly well for a guy who eats like a horse with a tapeworm and has the belly to show for it, beat us to the front porch. He peered in one of the long, narrow, beveled-glass sidelights framing either side of the door.

"Hell's bells, he has a gun!" Oscar announced, pulling out his own.

He tried the door, found it open, and barreled in. Mac and I were right behind.

The door opened right into a great room, with a big-screen TV on one wall and leather couch on the other. Oldendick and Westwood stood facing each other in the middle. The manager, looking gray and somehow deflated even though he hadn't lost any chins, was pointing a pistol at Westwood.

Oldendick has the gun. It's okay!

Or so I thought. I was about to get very confused.

"You have already made one mistake in taking a human life," said Mac. "Do not compound your error, I beg you."

He wasn't talking to Westwood.

Oldendick's attempted laugh rang hollow. "That's crazy! Chuck threatened me! I took the gun away from him. He killed Pargeter!"

That's what I thought.

"For what motive?" Oscar asked.

"How should I know!"

"And why did he threaten you?"

Oldendick wasn't a fast thinker. The best he could manage was, "He knew I saw him do it through the window of my office! I kept my mouth shut for the sake of the team, but he got worried that I would spill the beans when the season was over."

"Bullshit!" Westwood exploded. "I'm the dumbest guy on the planet for it to take me so long to figure out what happened. I knew from Moira and Freddie that Pargeter somehow learned about everything that happened in their house, but I never thought about what that could mean. When Moira told me that you suspected the place was bugged, it finally came to me in a flash: Pargeter must have picked up some of my phone calls with Bob. That meant he knew that Bob convinced me to take PEDs to get the extra oomph I needed to be a real power hitter. Going along with it was the stupidest mistake I ever made. I deserve whatever happens to me."

"That's a fantasy!" Oldendick croaked.

"And once you realized that Mr. Pargeter knew about the drugs," Mac told Westwood, "it was obvious to you that he must have been blackmailing your manager, a crime which hardly ever ends well for the perpetrator."

"Right. So, I came over here to tell him what I figured out. We've always been close, and I figured I could talk him into fessing up. Like I said, I'm the dumbest guy on the planet."

"Is that really your gun?" Oscar asked.

"No, sir."

"You ever touch it?"

"No."

"Then your prints won't be on it. And seeing as how it's a 9mm semi-auto—Taurus 709, isn't it?—there's a good chance it's the murder weapon."

"Which Mr. Oldendick fired out of his office window, having lured his victim there," Mac said. "Since that office is on the second floor, much closer to ground than the plaza level, he did not need to be an expert marksman to shoot successfully. Average ability was sufficient. I should have considered that possibility."

"Oh, hell!" Oldendick snapped. "If I give you the gun, will you just quit jabbering?"

"Hand it over slowly," Oscar said.

He did so.

"I never meant to hurt anybody," he said before Oscar could deliver the Miranda warning. "All I wanted was to manage a winning team. I've never been on a winning team. All those years in baseball, never a championship season. But I knew Chuck could lead the Eagles to one with a little help. You think he's the only one juicing? You think there's no juicing in the majors? Think again."

The old "everybody does it" defense.

"Thomas Pargeter threatened your dream," Mac prodded.

"He wanted more money than I had! Look around this place! Not a mansion, is it? You don't make a flipping fortune in the minors! And if I didn't pay up, Pargeter threatened to go to the cops. He would have done it, too, that obnoxious turd! I can't manage to feel all that bad about blowing him away." He looked at Westwood. "I do feel bad about you, though. I'm sorry I pulled you into this, Chuck. It's all my fault."

"No," Westwood said. "What I did is my fault. I bit the apple. You just offered it."

The screen door swung open behind us.

"I guess you don't need me," said Assistant Chief L. Jack Gibbons.

XV

Chuck Westwood sat out the remaining sixteen games of the season, plus the Liberty League division playoffs and the championship, but the Eagles took it all anyway. Oscar Hummel and Quincy Nicholson seemed almost equally pleased.

Westwood drew a suspended sentence under a plea deal because of his self-reporting and the limited time he used a drug called gamma-Butyrolactone (GBL).

Billy McAllister was the big star of post-season play, attracting the attention of major league scouts. There's a chance he may be wearing another uniform soon, this time under his own name. It's a good name.

Freddie Pargeter broke up with Roy Drinkwater, according to Popcorn, and has set her sights on winning a scholarship to Carnegie Mellon University. I saw Paul Baxter the other day when I gave blood. He told me to keep a certain date free. I could almost hear the wedding bells. Lynda says she told me so, but I don't recall that.

A McCabe-Cody Chronology

The month/year in which the primary action of each
adventure takes place

No Police Like Holmes	**April 2011**
Holmes Sweet Holmes	**September 2011**
The 1895 Murder	**May 2012**
"The Vatican Cameos" (in *The Disappearance of Mr. James Phillimore)*	**May 2012**
The Disappearance of Mr. James Phillimore	**June 2012**
"Art in the Blood" (in *Rogues Gallery)*	**October 2012**
"The Revengers" (in *Rogues Gallery)*	**October 2012**
"Santa Crime" (in *Rogues Gallery)*	**December 2012**
"A Cold Case" (in *Rogues Gallery)*	**April 2013**
"Dogs Don't Make Mistakes" (in *Rogues Gallery)*	**November 2013**
Bookmarked for Murder	**March 2015**
Erin Go Bloody	**March 2016**
Queen City Corpse	**April 2016**
"A Destination Murder" (in *Murderers' Row)*	**February 2017**
Death Masque	**May 2017**
"Dead on the Fourth of July (in *Murderers' Row)*	**July 2017**
Too Many Clues	**December 2018**
"Foul Ball" (in *Murderers' Row)*	**August 2019**

A Few Words of Thanks

The back of the book is the traditional place to offer thanks to those without whom the tome in hand would not be possible. That is a convention I follow only reluctantly, because back-of-the-book treatment seems hardly adequate.

For all their invaluable help in producing this eleventh McCabe-Cody volume, Jeff Cody and I wish to thank:

Ann Brauer Andriacco, my life-partner and co-conspirator;

Sharon Bohlen, for sharing her experiences as a rideshare driver;

Carlina de la Cova, for suggesting insulin as a murder weapon;

Mervin and Susan Marshall, for hosting us twice at their home in Barbados and for answering many questions about life on their island paradise;

Kieran McMullen, for once again patiently educating me about guns;

Jeff Suess, for proofreading and final preparation of the manuscript; and

Steve Winter, for giving the manuscript the incredible benefit of his engineering eye, as usual.

Any mistakes, however, are my own.

Publisher Steve Emecz and cover illustrator Brian Belanger remain the easiest collaborators any writer was ever so lucky to have.

About the Author

Dan Andriacco has been reading mysteries since he discovered Sherlock Holmes at the age of nine, and writing them almost as long.

The first ten Sebastian McCabe–Jeff Cody books are *No Police Like Holmes, Holmes Sweet Holmes, The* 1895 *Murder, The Disappearance of Mr. James Phillimore, Rogues Gallery* (shorter stories), *Bookmarked for Murder, Erin Go Bloody, Queen City Corpse, Death Masque,* and *Too Many Clues.* He is the co-author, with Kieran McMullen, of *The Amateur Executioner, The Poisoned Penman,* and *The Egyptian Curse* mysteries solved by Enoch Hale with Sherlock Holmes.

Also the author of *Baker Street Beat: An Eclectic Collection of Sherlockian Scribblings,* Dan is the leader of the Tankerville Club of Cincinnati and a member the Illustrious Clients of Indianapolis, the Agra Treasurers of Dayton, Watson's Tin Box of Ellicott City, the Sons of the Copper Beeches, and the Vatican Cameos—all scion societies of the Baker Street Irregulars. Follow Dan's long-running blog at www.danandriacco.com, his tweets at *@DanAndriacco,* and his Facebook Fan Page, Dan Andriacco Mysteries.

Dr. Dan and his co-conspirator, Ann Brauer Andriacco, have three grown children and six grandchildren. They live in Cincinnati, Ohio, USA, about forty miles downriver from Erin.

Praise for the McCabe–Cody mysteries

"With the McCabe and Cody mysteries, Dan Andriacco is doing for us what Conan Doyle did for the readers of Holmes and Watson in the late XIX century and early XX century: He's writing not only fantastic mystery stories but also creating unique characters that we can relate to, while admiring their adventures. *Too Many Clues* is another fantastic achievement in this series. Wonderful characters, amazing writing. Dan Andriacco is in great form."
　　—Nuno Robles, Lisbon, Portugal

"Again, Andriacco displays an encyclopedic memory for his enormous roster of clever and colorful characters. There is never a lull in his writing, and he propels his story to a surprising conclusion for this reader. *Death Masque* is another witty and lively novel by Andriacco."
　　—Writer Felicia Carparelli

"Dan Andriacco's *Queen City Corpse* is the latest in his series about Jeff Cody and Sebastian McCabe, who are in Cincinnati for a mystery convention and encounter mystery and murder, and a surprising solution; it's a lively story."
　　—Peter Blau in *Scuttlebutt from the Spermaceti Press*

"This *(Queen City Corpse)* is the seventh novel in a deliciously literate, witty series, with ingenious plots and engaging characters. Highly recommended!"
　　—*Sherlock Holmes Society of London*

"This *(Erin Go Bloody)* is Dan Andriacco's best book to date! I feel I could actually walk around downtown Erin, Ohio and not get lost. The characters are charming and believable. These are always entertaining reads!"
　　—Retired Sheriff Kenneth Ramsey, Sr.

"The ingenious twist at the end is an example of Andriacco's masterful ability to pen a page-turner. *Bookmarked for Murder* is a must-read for anyone who loves a classic who-done-it."
—Mystery writer Kathleen Kaska

"You're in the hands of a master of mystery plotting here. *Rogues Gallery* is a delightful read, hard to put down, and highly recommended. And did I say fun?"
—Screenwriter and novelist Bonnie MacBird

(*The Disappearance of Mr. James Phillimore*) "is a fun read in a series that keeps getting better with each new tale."
—Philip K. Jones

"*The* 1895 *Murder* is the most smoothly-plotted and written Cody/McCabe mystery yet. Mr. Andriacco plays fair with the reader, but his clues are deftly hidden, much as Sebastian McCabe hides the secrets to his magic tricks under an entertaining run of palaver."
—*The Well-Read Sherlockian*

"I loved Dan Andriacco's first novel about Sebastian McCabe and Jeff Cody, and I'm delighted to recommend (*Holmes Sweet Holmes*), which has a curiously topical touch."
—Roger Johnson, *Sherlock Holmes Society of London*

"*No Police Like Holmes* is a chocolate bar of a novel— delicious, addictive, and leaves a craving for more."
—*Girl Meets Sherlock*

Also from MX Publishing

Visit www.sherlockholmesbooks.com for dozens of other Sherlock Holmes novels, novellas, short story collections, Conan Doyle biographies, Holmes travel books, and more.

MX Publishing is the award-winning, world's largest independent Sherlock Holmes Book publishers with over 100 new authors and 500 new Sherlock Holmes stories in print.

www.ingramcontent.com/pod-product-compliance
Lightning Source LLC
Chambersburg PA
CBHW071313250626
47159CB00004B/1403